PAINLESS

PAINLESS

a novel

Jamie Mayer

THIS IS A GENUINE RARE BIRD BOOK

A Rare Bird Book | Rare Bird Books
453 South Spring Street, Suite 302
Los Angeles, CA 90013
rarebirdbooks.com

FIRST TRADE PAPERBACK ORIGINAL EDITION

Set in Minion Pro
Printed in the United States

Book Design by STARLING

10 9 8 7 6 5 4 3 2 1

Publisher's Cataloging-in-Publication data

Names: Mayer, Jamie C., author.
Title: Painless : a novel / Jamie Mayer.
Description: A Genuine Rare Bird Book | First Trade Paperback Original
Edition | Los Angeles, CA; New York, NY: Rare Bird Books, 2017.
Identifiers: ISBN 9781942600855
Subjects: LCSH Sensory disorders—Fiction. | People with disabilities—
Fiction. | Family—Fiction. | Love—Fiction. | Alcoholism—Fiction. |
Depression—Fiction. | Graphic novels—Fiction. | BISAC YOUNG ADULT
FICTION / Coming of Age
Classification: LCC PZ7.M4594 Pa 2017 | DDC [Fic—dc23

For my family

He has seen but half the universe who never has been shown the house of pain.

—Ralph Waldo Emerson

Do you feel what I feel?
Can we make that so it's part of the deal?

—Robbie Robertson, "Broken Arrow"

1. Quinn

I GOT HIT BY A car on the day my dad died. The stupid jackwagon in the BMW just kneecapped me—so it was fairly minor. I didn't feel a thing. Then again, I never do.

But hang on. Before I even say anything, shouldn't I say why I'm saying it? Isn't it kind of bizarre when you read a book and people start going "I did this," and "I thought that when such-and-whatever happened," and you're like "why are you telling me this stuff?" Well, I'm not just talking to talk, I'm telling you because I have to. I can't say the reason now because you won't believe me, but you'll eventually see what it is. Is that weird? What do I know, I don't even like books. Don't read 'em. What I do is draw pictures.

My eighth grade art teacher, Ms. Barnett, who was a whackadoodle in every other way—you can't take someone in homemade shoes seriously—said one thing I've always remembered. She said, "Every mentally healthy person creates art," even though they might not think of it as art. It might be the way they wash windows, if that's their job, or the way they raise their kids. She said art was anything you did that interpreted the world, something that reached out and communicated to other people, "Here's how I see things" or even, "Here's how I wish things were."

That was the last class I still bothered to go to before I just kinda stopped going to school altogether three years ago and no one even said anything. My mom was long gone. My dad was preoccupied, first just with being an angry bastard, and then with getting really really sick, and my older sister was too busy with her job and her husband and her kid, and taking care of my dad, and also totally fed up with me and my bullshit. So I just stopped going and no one cared. I don't mean to make my family seem worse than they are—why should they care if I finished high school when the doctors all told my parents I would probably never live to be an adult anyway? So you could see it like they were being nice by not making me sit in a classroom for my remaining days on earth. And, like any fourteen-year-old boy, I didn't want to go—so I didn't. But even three years later, I still remember that thing Ms. Barnett said. Though I'd change her description to say that both mentally healthy *and* totally screwed-up people make art, because I am compulsive. I can't stop drawing. Graphic novels and such. Though I'm not communicating anything to anybody, since I basically don't show them to anyone. Is it art if you draw a forest and no one sees it? So maybe she was right after all. The healthy people show their art.

Anyway, that's what I was doing before the car hit me. Sitting on our front steps in the crispy-brisk Boston sun, minding my own business, smoking my first cig of the day, listening to some rawk, and drawing the Shadow Man. He's my signature character. A big badass guy, shrouded in black—you never see his face, just slits for eyes.

This part of town had always been pretty rough—the only place my dad could buy a rowhouse on a fireman's salary—but the rich folks liked the cute little rowhouses and cobblestone streets, and started buying and renovating stuff, acting like their money might get moldy if they didn't spend it right away, and then got stuck here when the economy got weird, so now it's sort of this strange hybrid place. When I was a real little kid, it seemed like everyone's family had been here forever, their grandmas and uncles and cousins all lived here and always had. But now there's less of that. More BMWs. And the BMW drivers are pissed because their home values haven't risen enough to make them happy people, and the neighborhood is only half fancy. Maybe that's why that guy was driving so dickishly.

The front of our house—where I was living with my dying dad, my sister Caitlin, and her husband and kid—was directly across the street from the concrete yard of an elementary school. Same school I went to. Same-but-different saggy teachers chatting with each other while the same-but-different snot-nosed kids pummeled each other at recess inside that same chain-link fence. And that morning, a particularly scrawny kid was being chased by other kids who were yelling words you'd like to think fourth graders don't know—but come on, they do. So I turned the music in my headphones up to keep it out, because I was trying to get this panel of Shadow Man right— which is why I didn't hear the front door opening behind me. First clue I had that someone was there was my headphones being ripped off my head.

"Quinn, I said listen to me!"

It was Caitlin. Not even 9:00 a.m. and she was already mad at me.

"I'm busy."

"He asked—nicely—for you to please come up and talk to him."

"I doubt that."

"You know he can't come down."

"I don't like going up there."

"Come on—"

"I just lit this."

I took a long drag on my cig for dramatic emphasis, even though I knew it would piss her off even more. She hates that I smoke—she has to, she's a nurse, so it's like official policy, even though I'll probably never get old enough to get lung cancer so who cares—but she gave up fighting with me about it a long time ago. Besides, I was pretty sure she was lying about our dad wanting to see me. We didn't talk, my dad and me; the feeling was mutual. I couldn't even remember the last time I spoke to him, definitely before he got sick. Even before that I didn't have anything to say to him. He had a lot to say to me—or at me— when I was growing up, especially after my mom was gone— mostly stuff about what a terrible kid I was—and I just stopped talking back. Rage deflector shield up. Eventually, he gave up on me and I think we were both relieved. We lived like silent parallel lines, always aware of the other's position, but never intersecting. So when Cait told me he suddenly wanted to talk, I called bullshit. I guess it was possible he had some pent-up rage he wanted to vent at me before he died, but I wasn't up for that either.

After a long pause, Caitlin just shut the door. Score one for me.

"Chicken! Bawwwwk bukbukbuk!" Over on the playground, glittering with recess commotion, the scrawny kid finally got tripped by a bigger boy, and a punching, flailing pile of followers urged on top of him. From under the pile, the kid looked over at me and saw me watching him get the snot beat out of him. Wasn't much I could do. There was a fence between us and anyway I could already see the recess teacher slow-jogging toward the scene.

The jerkwad BMW was still a few minutes away from racing down our street, and my dad hadn't died yet. I just sat there, not knowing how much things were about to change, took a deep drag on my cig, and appreciated the hell out of the way the wisps of smoke curlicued lazily into the autumn air.

2. Caitlin

AITLIN'S SENSIBLE NURSE SHOES squeaked as she crossed the kitchen linoleum. She stopped in front of the coffee maker, pulled out the glass pot, and poured herself a third mug as the machine hissed and sizzled, scolding her for taking it out too soon. She sipped at it and leaned over the kitchen sink to see Quinn through the window.

He wasn't making any moves to get up off the front steps, just sat there with his head bent over his sketchbook in a cloud of smoke. Despite the fact that 90 percent of the time she just wanted to smack him, she still loved the expression on his face when he was drawing. Not peaceful, exactly, but unconflicted. Concentrating. He had the same fair complexion and shockingly dark hair and eyelashes as their mother had had—and that Caitlin had, too, except she didn't have any of the scars and tattoos Quinn had accumulated on his pale skin. Black Irish, people often said when they saw them as kids, nodding as though that explained something.

"Morning, baby." Her husband Will, half-dressed for the firehouse, gave her a peck on the cheek but she barely registered it as she peered out the kitchen window again to see if Quinn had moved from his stoop perch. He hadn't.

"Your dad sounded worse last night," said Will. "Thought he was gonna hack up a lung."

"I know. Is Winnie ready for school?"

"She wants her purple dress." Will picked through the laundry in the clothes dryer with determination, and Caitlin sighed because he seemed to see all of life's problems as physical obstacles to be pushed aside, broken down, overcome. It was a quality that she both loved and was irritated by.

"Can't she wear something else?"

"You know how she is when she gets her mind fixed on something. It's purple or bust." Will pulled a preschool-size, berry-stained purple dress from the mountain of unwashed clothes on the floor in front of the washing machine. "Shit, Cait, I thought you did laundry."

Caitlin ignored the comment, not wanting to start a thing at this insufficiently-caffeinated hour, and instead banged on the window to get Quinn's attention, gesturing like a crazy lady as she yelled through the glass, "Upstairs!"

✖

HIS HORRIFIC CHOKING COUGH didn't sound like it could be coming from such a hollowed-out, withered man. He looked easily twenty years older than he was—which was only fifty-six. He lay half-sunken in the rumpled sheets, half-alive, surrounded by the clinical paraphernalia of the dying. Prescription bottles, oxygen tanks with their snaky tubing, plastic receptacles for every imaginable bodily fluid. The cough again, violent enough to crack a rib.

"What the fuck—" Coughing. "What the fuck does he want to say to me?"

"I don't know, Dad, I just know he wanted to come talk to you." Caitlin came out of the bathroom with a freshly rinsed pee vessel and placed it matter-of-factly on his bedside table.

Working as a nurse made her almost immune to the weirdness of doing things like this for her own father, but not completely.

"Why?"

"I don't know. But try to be nice when he comes in, okay? You two might have some things to say to each other."

"Not today."

Photos and medals covered the wall behind his bed, proof of healthier days. A group photo of the guys at the firehouse where he'd worked his whole career. Him getting an award. A large picture of him in full uniform, arm around Caitlin's husband Will, also in his fire gear. Only one older family photo showed him with his wife and two children, all together in the same frame. Only the two kids, standing in front of the rowhouse steps, were looking at the camera—an awkward, preteen Caitlin with two giant front teeth and a goofy smile, and an Ace-bandaged Quinn, just three, staring unsmiling into the lens. Mom, behind them, glancing off to the side, spiritless and distracted. Dad, alongside, gazing over at her with a stern expression. It felt to Caitlin like all these photos of her father, ghosts of his former, physically imposing self, were drifting above his now gaunt head like nervous party guests, wondering if it was time to leave.

"How's the pain, Dad? Do you want the Dilaudid?"

"For Christ's sake, leave me alone with the pills. No more nothing." He coughed again, wincing in pain.

"I'll get these refilled for you anyway." She pocketed the vial. "Father Connell wanted to know if he should come by."

"Fuck no. Give me a cigarette."

"No, Dad."

He struggled to grab the pack off the nightstand. Resigned, she wheeled his oxygen tank away from the bed, then handed him a cigarette. As she reached across and lit it for him, he gripped her wrist, a sudden vise, surprising her with his strength.

"Don't let him do it, Caity. Don't let him do it to you, too," he growled.

It took her a moment to digest his outburst before she pulled free of his grip. "The day nurse should be here soon. I've got to get dressed for work."

She ducked into the bathroom, with its old claw-footed tub and unrenovated avocado-colored tile, avoided looking at herself in the stained medicine cabinet mirror, and popped a Dilaudid pill into her mouth with a hurried tap water chaser. Better.

3. Quinn

OH, HERE WE GO.

After the recess teacher extracted the scrawny kid from the bottom of the pileup and walked him off to the nurse's office, the Big Kid who had started it all needed to stir up something else, so there he was, hands hooked into the chainlink, idly kicking the base of the fence and staring across the street at me.

"Hey! I'm talking to you, hey!" he yelled.

I sighed. Nine years old and already an asshole. Some of his little followers joined him at the fence, glancing over at me and whispering to each other.

"You wanna see something cool?" the Big Kid ventured.

I looked behind and all around me, making a show of it, pretending I didn't know he was talking to me.

"Just come here. Check this out."

"What, you guessed your dad's porn site password, but you need someone to explain what you're looking at?"

"Duh, no. Just come here, you gotta see this."

I didn't have anything better to do, so I moseyed across the street and up to the school fence. The Big Kid held out a jar with a herd of pissed-off red ants inside. A littler, orange-haired Sidekick pushed to the front of the pack, cupping a squirming frog in his dirty hands. Enacting some silent, creepy, ritual, the pack of kids spread out, forming a half circle around the Big Kid and the Sidekick.

Making sure I was watching, they set the jar of ants down on the asphalt, took off the lid and clumsily jammed the frog inside, screwing the lid down after. For a few, desperate moments, the frog leaped around inside the jar, pounding its poor, dumb frog head against the tin lid. Then, it stopped and sat there, accepting the instant tide of tiny, stinging ants. It just stared, motionless, Zen frog, and finally seemed to deflate, beaten. A small chorus of awe rippled around the little semicircle. The Big Kid looked over to me for a reaction.

"Well, that's quite the all-American pastime you guys have got going on there." I knew that wasn't the response he wanted—which is why I gave it. I'm a jerk like that, I guess.

He tilted his head and nodded his chin toward my front door. "You live in that house?"

Duh. I just came from there, wiseass. You see me sitting there every day.

"I bet you wouldn't stick your hand in this jar," he asked.

"I bet I wouldn't too."

"But you could, though, couldn't you?"

I froze for a second, my stomach contracting into a tight ball as I realized where he was going with this. I turned and headed back to the house.

"Chicken," he called out.

Me? I spun around, trying to laugh it off, still walking backward across the street. "Kid, give it up—don't you have some milk money to extort?"

And that's when it happened.

Jackwagon BMW came banging around the corner, saw me and blared his horn—so thoughtful!—as he screeched to a stop. But he stopped about six inches too late, and kneecapped me, folding me over the hood of his car. Bashed my face pretty good. And as I slowly stood up, all I could hear was the *drip drip* of the blood leaking from my nose and sizzling on the hot metal of his hood.

Time slowed as I stared right at the driver, the windshield between us. His "oh shit" face frozen in place as his brain flashed through his options. No doubt he would have just taken off like a bottle rocket if I hadn't been standing up against his front bumper.

Over on my front steps, I distinctly heard the pages of my drawing pad flip and flutter in the wind. I knew what that meant. I looked over and saw Shadow Man looming, seven feet tall, pointing his shadowy finger right at the driver and ordering his snarling black shadow dog to attack.

My eyes narrowed. I pivoted and kicked out the BMW's left headlight. Then turned and nailed the other one. That felt a little better.

"Watch where you're going, asshat—there are little kids in this neighborhood."

I could sense that the clump of kids was still standing at the fence watching me, so I turned and looked the Big Kid in the eye—he stared back for a moment, stunned, like he was afraid I might turn my freaky superhero durability against him somehow, then bolted, followed by the rest of the pack of kids.

I headed back to my steps. The BMW screeched off. I noticed that the Sidekick was still lingering at the fence, squinting at me and nervously coiling a piece of his orange hair around his thumb—and it bugged me for some reason. I pointed my finger at him like a gun and made a low shooting nose. It worked and the kid took off running.

I walked up the steps, collecting my papers and scattered pens. A red drop spattered down on my drawing pad and I remembered about the bleeding. Damn. I dabbed at my nose with my sleeve, and headed inside to draw in peace.

4. Caitlin

"**I** CAN ONLY DEAL WITH one thing at a time," Caitlin said to Will, hushed, as if keeping the volume down could hide the blade in her voice. She dumped some whisked eggs into a pan and slid the empty bowl into the sink. Will had been relatively cool about living here with her dad and brother, especially since the end was clearly approaching with her dad. It had never made any sense for them to get their own place. Not with her nursing school loans to pay off; but even more so after Dad had gotten sick, with her having to spend more and more time taking care of him, and since the house would eventually be theirs after he had passed.

For months now, it had felt like the end was clearly approaching. It was lung cancer Dad had, which had recently spread to his pericardium, the double-layered lining that surrounds the heart. The space between the layers is filled with a fluid that protects the heart from external shocks. When Caitlin learned about this in nursing school, she was fascinated, imagining how life's ups and downs might affect this lining, might help puff it up to better buffer the threats that lurked in each new day, or whittle away at it, thinning and making it liable to pop, leaving the heart exposed and defenseless.

But as her dad's illness dragged on and on, Quinn just rubbed Will more and more the wrong way, and Will was perpetually on her case about getting more on her brother's case—to get him to do something, anything, other than sitting around drawing "cartoons." She couldn't really defend Quinn—Will was right—but his constant irritation really wore on her. What was she supposed to do? A normal person would have their hands full with just a four-year-old and a marriage that needed "work" and a sick-as-hell dad. Oh yeah, and a demanding full-time job. Then add in Quinn and his "issues" as their mom had always called his condition? That's when she just closed her eyes, swallowed a pill, and hoped it would all sort itself out.

Quinn slouched into the kitchen from outside. Will, gathering up his gear for work, shot him an annoyed look but Quinn pretended not to see and just walked over to pour himself a cup of coffee. Before taking a sip, he automatically held it out toward Caitlin and she dipped her finger in his mug to check the temperature.

"Fine." Caitlin turned back to the stove where she finished hastily scrambling the eggs, scraping most of them onto a plastic child's plate and eating the rest right out of the pan with the wooden spoon, brushing stray egg crumbs off her pale green nurse scrubs. One less plate to clean—efficiency.

Quinn took his coffee and headed toward the door to his basement room. Winnie galloped into the kitchen in her stained purple dress, tackling him before he could reach the safety of his room. "Uncle Quinn, your hair's really really messy!"

"Well, so is yours, monkey face." Quinn scribbled his hand across her head and she screamed with delight and adoration.

"Shhh, no yelling, Win. Grandpa's trying to rest." Will scooped Winnie up and away from Quinn, swinging her onto his brawny shoulders. He caught Quinn's eye. "Uncle Quinn doesn't have to brush his hair—because he doesn't have to go to work or school or *anything.*"

"*Will,*" warned Caitlin. "Not now. Come on, Winnie, come eat your eggs."

Quinn ignored Will's dig and started down the stairs to his basement room. Caitlin followed.

"Wait." She reached down and gently put a hand on Quinn's shoulder and he reflexively twitched away from her touch. "Can you just think about going upstairs?"

"I thought about it."

Her eyes drifted down to the slowly-spreading patch of blood on one of the knees of his jeans.

"What happened?"

"Nothing, I just tripped. I'm fine"

She noticed a fresh stream of blood trickling from his nostril. "And your nose! It could be broken."

"It's not broken…" His voice pitched high, making light of it.

"How would you know? Caitlin shook her head, seething. "I don't believe it—this is the second time this week. I can't leave you alone for a second." She grabbed his arm. "You're coming with me to the hospital."

Quinn wrestled his arm away. "Come on Nurse Ratched, just patch me up."

God she hated when he called her that. "Don't be a smart-ass."

"Isn't that better than a dumb ass?"

She grabbed a handful of his shirt and pulled him up the stairs back into the kitchen.

"I don't need to go, okay? *I don't fucking need to go!*"

Startled at his fierce tone, Caitlin stepped back involuntarily. She felt her face get hot and tried to hold it together, but tears silently, disobediently rolled down her cheeks.

Will took a heavy step toward Quinn. "You do *not* talk to her like that."

"Will, stop," said Caitlin. She turned to Quinn. "I'm taking you to the hospital." And back to Will. "Can you drop Winnie off at school?"

Winnie's lower lip trembled. "I don't want Daddy to take me, I want Mommy to take me."

"What about your dad?" Will asked, "The daytime nurse isn't here yet."

"Shit. Okay, then wait until she comes? Win will just have to be late for school." Will rolled his eyes. More points against Quinn the Disrupter.

"I don't wanna be late for school," Winnie whimpered.

Caitlin gave Winnie a quick hug, told her it would be okay, and pulled Quinn toward the door. "Let's go."

"Cait, I'm telling you it's nothing. It's fine, I'm fine."

"It's not fine, you're not fine, nothing about this is fine, and you're the last person who would know what fine even was."

"It's just not a big deal…"

She maneuvered Quinn out the door and shut it behind them.

Through the door came the sound of Winnie bursting into tears. "I want Mommy!" The sound of her sobs faded as Caitlin marched Quinn away from the house and into the car, but she could still feel their echoes silently scraping at the lining of her heart as she put the key in the ignition and headed off to the hospital.

5. Quinn

"SO WHAT HAPPENED THIS time, Quinn?"

Doctor Silverman was shining his penlight into my eye, so all I could see was a ring of wispy hair with a white flare where his face should've been. It was sort of a cool effect, and made me think of a new character I could draw, a man who glowed so hard he blinded people.

"Quinn!" Caitlin stood in the corner, arms folded. "Tell him."

"Nothing. A car hit me."

"Hate when that happens," said Silverman. What a wise guy. I'd seen him like twenty or thirty times before, he was always trying to buddy-buddy me and it was annoying. Most of the ER docs got jokey like that, actually—I guess it was just how people dealt with seeing crazy shit all day—but Silverman irked me the most for some reason.

He took my right arm and started working his way down, pressing with his thumbs, feeling the structure to see if anything was broken. My right wrist was swollen and pink, and he rotated it around slowly, like it might hurt me, but of course it didn't.

✖

I DON'T REALLY LIKE to talk about it, but let's just get this out of the way. I don't feel pain. It's a neurological thing, pretty rare, I was born this way. Most kids like this don't live very long—they chew their own tongue to bits, or break a leg but keep walking on it.

When you're little, you don't really get why it's not a good idea to yank big handfuls of hair out of your scalp—or jump off your roof. Hurting yourself—or other people—is just an abstract, intellectual concept that you have to learn to not do; there's no instinctive aversion like everyone else has. I've been to the emergency room more times than I can count. As a kid, I was covered in bruises and almost always had a cast on some part of my body or another. When I was four, child protective services took me away from my parents because a neighbor thought they must be abusing me. After I walked up and pressed my palms to the side of my foster dad's barbecue grill, watching calmly as my skin blackened and peeled off, they realized something else was going on, and soon I was my parents' headache again.

✖

A NURSE CAME IN with X-rays and put them up on the light board. She must've been new, I'd never seen her, and she had this crazy constellation of birthmarks splotched across her face that I kept staring at, trying to pick out images like you would with clouds drifting across the sky. She saw me looking and I decided to not look away, just to see what would happen. I wondered if she would recognize that we were fellow freaks. I guess not because after a few seconds she scooted out the door mumbling something to Silverman about needing to fetch some test results.

"Nothing broken, at least," said Silverman, peering at my bones on the light board. He turned to Caitlin. "Maybe a hairline on that right wrist—definitely sprained it pretty badly. You've really got to look after it. Ice it every two hours, anti-inflammatories."

"Tell him," she said, annoyed. Typical Cait. Pissed at me for making her late for work, but she was the one who made me come here in the first place; I knew it was a minor thing. He just said it wasn't broken. Maybe she was mad because I'd been right, that it was no big deal. Her phone rang and she left the room.

Silverman strapped an air brace on my right wrist. "Keep that on for at least four weeks to make sure it heals, and don't use it for anything—I mean *anything*... Know what I mean...?" He gave me a weird eyebrow jump, that buddy thing again. "...Or you'll really hurt it and you'll wind up back here."

Was he really referring to me beating off? Wow, kind of inappropriate, Doc. But I just said, "What about drawing? That's my drawing hand."

"Oh right, you do those comics. Yeah, lay off the drawing for a month."

No way I could not draw for four weeks—it was a compulsion. I could barely go two hours without at least a little Shadow Man sketch on an envelope or something. If I couldn't hold a pencil with the air cast on, I'd just have to take it off when I was drawing, and try to remember to put it back on after.

Caitlin always treated the doctor's orders like they were the word of God, like I had to take every pill at the precise minute it was supposed to be taken, apply the ice for the exact number of minutes they had said, as though I would just utterly fail to heal if I didn't. But "orders" was such a fascistic word. I liked to think of them as recommendations, like a jazz player might glance at the sheet music once and then take off on his own interpretation. I was the Thelonious Monk of my body, man—I experimented, I improvised, I be-bopped around, finding out what happened if I did this, or didn't do that, wandering far from the written score and then making my way back to safety, one healed body part at a time. Ahh, I'm just making shit up now. Mainly, I'm just too lazy or stubborn to do exactly what they say. It all seems to heal up eventually anyway. One day, I'm sure it won't—but that can only happen once, right? For now, I'm gonna keep drawing.

6. Caitlin

C AITLIN HAD RECEIVED AND ignored two calls from Will while she'd been in with the doctor and Quinn; they'd had to wait for radiology to come down and do the X-rays and it had taken forever. She thought everyone who worked at the hospital should experience being on the patient's end of things sometime. How could they keep Quinn sitting in a room for an hour waiting for a radio tech to come in when she was late for her shift? And that was probably the speed treatment because they knew she worked there. She'd hadn't been a nurse that long, but everyone knew about her brother because they'd been in dozens of times over the years.

So when her cell phone rang for third time, she excused herself to take it, mainly as a way to get out of the tiny windowless room where Quinn was on her last nerve. As she stepped into the hall, on the second ring, a pear-shaped hospital administrator came angling straight toward her.

"There you are. Aren't you working today?"

Caitlin hit the "ignore" button on the phone and squeezed out a pained "what are you gonna do?" smile and a shrug. "Family emergency...my brother." *It is so odd when men are pear-shaped*, she thought.

"Ah. Listen, you didn't hear this from me, but your name came up in the department meeting the other day...the missed days, last minute schedule changes..." He laced his hands behind his back and rocked back and forth on his heels in a display of pear-ish compassion.

"I know, I know, I'm working on it," said Caitlin. "Between my brother and my dad right now, it's been difficult."

"You don't need to explain to me—I'm just trying to do you a favor by letting you know what's in the air... I'll see you upstairs."

"I've got to take my brother home first."

"Can he take the T?"

"It's like three buses to get to our neighborhood from here and it only comes every forty-five minutes or so and—"

"I'd hurry. Just saying."

The administrator gave her a quick sympathetic smile and strode off. Caitlin sighed. Nothing worse than a scolding wrapped in the cloak of kindness. She glanced at her phone. Two voicemails from Will. Who had time to listen to voicemails? He was probably wondering what to pack for Winnie's lunch or something—just figure it out, Will. She'd call him when they were done. She tried to remember who her shift boss was today—if it was Britta, it was gonna be a long day. Jesus, was Quinn done yet?

7. Quinn

"**Y**OUR SISTER SAYS THIS is happening more and more." Silverman peered through his reading glasses at my chart, which was as thick as a Bible. "It looks like this is your seventh or eighth time in the ER this year—last year you were only in a couple of times—any thoughts about why it's escalated?"

"This was an accident, okay? It wasn't intentional. That's why they call them 'accidents.'"

"You know what I mean, Quinn. You really don't have much leeway for accidents. You've got to live your life in a way that prevents you from getting injured in the first place…"

I just shut him out, got off the table, and started getting dressed. Ambushing a guy for some "serious" conversation when he's still sitting in his boxers is so not the way to do it.

"You know, I'm not trying to scare you—that's just the reality of your condition." Seeing that he wasn't making any headway, he flipped through my file, trying a different tack. I should've seen this one coming. "Maybe you should go back to talk to this…Dr. Engels for a few sessions?"

Yeah, right. I was so out of there.

8. Caitlin

AITLIN DROVE QUINN HOME from the hospital in silence. He stared out the window, beating out an internal drum rhythm on his thigh. She gripped the wheel in silence, eyes straight ahead, trying to will the traffic lights to break her way so she could just drop him home and quickly weave her way back to the hospital, where at least it was clear what was expected of her. Her mind raced with complaints and criticisms and *and-another-thing*s, but she didn't have it in her for an argument, so vowed to keep her mouth shut. That lasted about eight seconds.

"Why are you *like* this?" she erupted.

"Just lucky I guess."

She threw him a stabby look; it was the sarcasm more than the physical calamities that drove her up the wall.

"I was born this way—what's *your* excuse?"

She took a deep breath and tried to be the grown-up. The fucking mom. She was only seven years older, why did she have to be the mom? Because their mom had bailed on them. Yeah, but still. She was twenty-five but had been acting like his mom for half her life.

"You know what I mean. You can't... What are you *thinking*?" It wasn't just an empty question—she really wanted to know. It seemed like it should be a simple equation. You have X condition so you can't do Y dangerous things. It was like he was constantly forgetting he had it. Or didn't care.

Quinn just kept his head turned toward the window.

9. Quinn

WHAT *WAS* I THINKING when things like that happened? I tried to get my head around her question without really letting her know that I was. I did really want to know. Maybe if I just *thought* about it, I could uncover it. No, no, no, that was a stupid idea. That kind of thinking hurt my brain. I turned toward her, wanting to convey this dilemma somehow, but couldn't find any way to explain what seemed so simple in my head a moment before. So I didn't say anything.

She must've thought I was just ignoring her question, because she jumped on me like a rabid dingo. "Are you *trying* to piss me off? Are you *trying* to drive me fucking crazy?"

I suddenly found the hole in the thigh of my jeans fascinating. "This has got to change, this—"

Her rant trailed off as we turned into our street. An ambulance and a couple of fire trucks were double-parked in front of our house, their red lights mutely revolving.

"Oh no..." Caitlin parked on a diagonal and jumped out, running ahead. I stayed in the car, taking it in. Watching through the windshield it felt like someone had turned the sound down on the world. Will came out of the house, carrying Winnie. He said something to Caitlin and hugged her. She cried on his shoulder. Winnie cried, too, without quite knowing why. It was a silent movie. Maybe I could stay in the car forever. Caitlin glanced back at me and I considered my options.

I hiked my knapsack up onto my shoulder and got out of the car, drifting toward the house as the sounds of reality slowly ramped up. I sort of kept my distance, idling around the periphery of the action, staying a good six feet away from anyone or anything.

A couple of older firemen, guys my dad had worked with, came out of the house and approached Caitlin.

"Caity, honey, I'm so sorry..." said the one with a silvery crew cut as he pulled her into a big hug. I couldn't remember his name.

Another one awkwardly nodded to me. "Sorry about your dad."

"Yeah," I said quietly.

After a moment, Caitlin pulled away from silvery crew cut, wiping her tears, shifting into practical mode.

"I've got to call people. The funeral home, Aunt Dorothy... Quinn, come inside with me."

"Nah, I'm going out"

"Out where?" Will spat.

"Out."

"Let him go." Caitlin didn't have it in her to fight with me. I started inching away.

Will whirled his outrage around toward her. "That's bullshit! Jesus, Cait—"

She dug in her purse and shoved a twenty-dollar bill at me. "I know you'll go out no matter what I say, so you may as well save me a trip and pick up some food. There'll be people coming over, we'll need food."

"People will bring food," argued Will.

"We need *something* to give them." She turned back to me. "Get a couple of pounds of ground beef, I'll make a meatloaf."

I took the cash and made a break for it, wedging the crumpled twenty into the front pocket of my jeans, zipping my beat-up old leather jacket all the way up and tucking my chin into my scarf to fend off the chill.

As I walked, she called out after me. "Don't go to the market—go to the butcher shop on Hanover—and don't let them give you the stuff in the case, make them grind it fresh!"

Yeah, sure, got it. I just kept walking.

"Cait, the last thing you need to deal with is cooking," said Will.

"Don't tell me what I need to deal with," snapped Caitlin.

I turned the corner at the end of the street, making the chaos recede behind me.

✷

THIS WAS THE HEART of the old Italian community. The new arrivals shopped at the Whole Foods a few streets over, but the grandmas still shopped here, where the shop owners winched out shabby striped awnings and set up bins of fruits and vegetables along the sidewalk every morning. You could still see kids in parochial school uniforms at Ernesto's Pizza every day after school, eating giant slices off greasy paper plates. The once-busy Sons of Italy Social Club was hanging on—a few old men with deeply-lined faces sat backward in vinyl covered chairs on the sidewalk in front, arguing in Italian—maybe about what would become of their fully-paid off building once they were all gone. Some of these wood and brick buildings—storefronts on the street level, with another floor or two of apartments above—had been staring at each other across these narrow streets for more than three hundred years.

I walked through the neighborhood. Here and there, someone would know me just from seeing me around and give a friendly wave, but after I'd passed by, more than a few turned to each other to whisper.

I didn't pay much attention to that kind of thing anymore, but I did notice a large black wolfy dog with even blacker eyes keeping pace with me along the other side of the street, looking across at me. I stopped walking; the dog stopped, sat, and stared.

"Here, boy. Come 'ere."

The dog stayed on the other side of the street, but when I started walking again, the dog followed from a distance, never taking his eyes off me.

I turned into the door of Steve's Komix, pulling my notebook out of my backpack.

10. Quinn

"**H**EY, ASSHOLE." THIS WAS how Steve always greeted me. A term of endearment.

I replied with the traditional response: "Fuck off."

I don't know how he stayed in business. He was too nice, letting the kids who were late for or skipping school sit on the floor, flipping through back issues as long as they wanted without buying anything. Plus, the place was organized in a way only Steve could comprehend—comics were stacked on shelves, overflowing out of boxes. Probably held the record for most books per square inch. He was sitting on a stool behind the counter, reading some lame vampire comic.

"What're you reading," I asked, "girl shit?"

His fleshy face turned pink with embarrassment. "Miranda thinks I should stock it, broaden the customer base." Miranda was his girlfriend, and he pretty much did what she told him. I think he was just so thrilled to be a chubby comic book guy with a girlfriend, he didn't wanna blow it. "But whatever—where have you been?" Steve asked. He nodded at my sketchbook. "A hundred bucks says you haven't finished it yet, am I right?"

"I have more sketches I can show you."

"Forget sketches. I needed a finished book to show the guy at DC. I've told him it was coming for so long, he stopped calling me. I bet it's probably too late now anyway."

"Whatever. I don't even know if I'd want to show it."

"All I've seen are a few early panels. For all I know, that's all you've got."

"It's pretty much all done except for the ending. I basically know what happens, I'm just not sure how to do it."

"Tell me—I'll help you figure it out."

"Nah."

He was starting to sweat a little bit, just itching to see my work. I don't know why but that made me feel nervous, too. Part of me wanted to show him; I mean, he was pretty much the only other person I knew who cared about this stuff. But the thought of showing my drawings to anyone at all, even him, made my stomach flip over.

Steve shrugged. "I mean, at this point, I don't care, I just thought I could help a brother out." His fake nonchalance was pretty funny. I took a deep breath, opened my notebook and paged to my character designs. Steve almost tripped over himself trying to clear the mess of comics off the counter to make a spot for me to put down my book.

"This is the main character, the hunter, who I think I showed you before."

"Shadow Man?"

"Right."

"Human?"

"Not really. He's sacrificed his humanity to be a vigilante, to protect society. He's a real badass—intimidating as all crap. That's his attack dog." I pointed to the Shadow Man's dog, and it suddenly occurred to me that the dog looked more than a little like the wolfy-looking one that had followed me down the street. I wondered for a second if I had maybe seen that dog in the neighborhood before, though, I didn't remember ever seeing it, and had subconsciously called up it when I first drew the attack dog. *Yeah*, I thought, *that's probably what happened.*

I flipped the page to a different character, a small, feral, sooty creature with glowing demon's eyes.

"So Shadow Man's hunting down this Boy Demon, who's gotten loose," I continued.

"Special powers?"

"Chaos incarnate. He basically incinerates everything he touches. Killed his own parents, everything around him."

"Excellent!" Steve cackled. "Bad seed, raised by wolves!"

"Yeah, kind of. A real monster."

"So the ending seems easy enough—Shadow Man kills the demon kid... I mean it depends what you have in mind for future episodes..."

While Steve talked, I focused on my drawing of the demon boy, trying his suggestion on in my mind, ways to kill him, how it might go down, when all of a sudden it felt like the world dropped three inches, then caught itself. I looked around—had there been an earthquake or something?—but no one else seemed to have noticed. Cross-legged kids were still quietly reading. The jingle bells on the door hadn't budged. I looked down at my sketchbook again, at the evil demon boy, who was spinning, snarling, shooting fireballs from his hands. And then the drawing moved. Effing moved! The fireball flew across the page! I looked over at Steve, who was still obliviously chatting away.

"...because if you want to keep him around, maybe Shadow Man could just throw him back into demon jail, or banish him to another planet or something."

I reached over to shut the notebook, trying not to look at it again. "Yeah, it's gotta be something like that, but for some reason, I can't make it work right. I need to think about it some more."

As I leaned across, Steve noticed the air cast on my wrist. "What happened to your hand, man?"

"Nothing, just a sprain. You know, I remembered something I gotta do—I'll catch you later."

"That's not your drawing hand, is it?"

I was already out the door. He called after me.

"Oh, for Christ's sake...let *me* draw the freaking thing! It'll look like shit, but at least it'll be done!"

The door jangled shut behind me and I stopped short. The wolfy dog was across the cobblestone street, looking straight at me. It suddenly freaked me out how much it looked like the Shadow Man's dog. I started walking away down the sidewalk and the dog followed on a parallel path.

11. Quinn

THE DRIED BLOOD ON the necks of the ducks that hung from the row of iron hooks in the window at Raffallo's Butcher Shop always fascinated me as a kid. It was evidence that they had been real ducks, alive and quacking, probably minding their own duck business before suddenly meeting their violent end. This place had been here forever, and my sister shopped here, just like my mom used to. I hadn't been inside in years—but I remembered the ducks.

That day, there was also a single lean, gray rabbit hanging in the window, limp as an unloved puppet.

"It's a little over, that okay?"

The owner's son, a thick-necked guy with a buzz cut, stood shifting his weight impatiently behind the counter, a little bloody heap of ground beef piled on the scale.

Damn, I'd forgotten to tell him. I turned away from the rabbit. "I'm sorry, could I get it ground fresh?"

"Ground fresh?" He was annoyed, but what else was he doing, I was the only customer in here.

"Yeah, sorry. It's on accounta my sister. That's what she wanted."

"It'll cost extra."

"Yeah, whatever, fine."

He lumped the meat back into the case and poked his head into the back room. "Pop, I need two poundsa ground beef!"

An unseen, gravelly Italian accent responded, "What, they don't want what's already ground?"

"No."

"It'll cost extra," the accent said.

Meathead turned to me with a told-you-so smile. "Anything else?"

"No. Actually, yeah. I was wondering if I could maybe get some bones or something for my dog." I glanced out the door— the black dog was sitting patiently across the street, like he was waiting for me.

"I'm afraid I can't just do that. See, due to the fact that people *buy* them to make soup with, I can't just *give* 'em away." He was being so condescending, it made me seriously consider punching him in his big square head...but then I saw over his shoulder, through the door to the back room, a glimpse of the butcher, his father, carving hunks off of a huge slab of beef and dropping them into a grinder. Real flesh, real blood, the knife so shiny and sharp...

"Do you want to frickin' buy some or not?" Meathead pulled my attention back to the front counter.

"What? Yeah, sure. I'll buy two. Thanks, champ." Ooh, he hated me calling him that. If I'd drawn a picture of him right at that moment, I'd have put poofy jets of steam coming out his ears.

✖

I WALKED OUT OF the butcher shop, zipping Caitlin's package of meat into the front pocket of my knapsack and rattling the paper bag of bones I'd bought for the black dog.

"Bones, I got fresh bones. It's your lucky day."

No sign of him. I stood there for a minute, whistled, scanned up and down the street, but he was gone.

"Your loss."

I tossed the bag into a trash barrel and kept walking.

12. Quinn

Z *IP, ZIP, ZIP!*

I looked over in the shadowy corner of the bar and saw three darts crowding a cork bull's-eye. A hipster chick high-fived her bulls-eye-hitting teammate, a punk rock girl with tough makeup and delicate features. Punk Rock Girl's accomplishment was also applauded by their opponents, some bearded bikers. When a neighborhood joint gets discovered by bohemian posers, it makes for some weird darts partners—but beer smoothes over the differences.

I sat on a stool at one end of the bar, empty glass in front of me. No one here had questioned my age in the year I'd been coming in here. Maybe I'd been a fixture in the neighborhood for so long, people just assumed I was older than I was. Or left me alone because they felt bad for me or something. I was trying to doodle on my napkin, trying to find a way to hold a pen in my drawing hand but the air cast made it really tough. I ripped open the Velcro and took it off.

I tried to ignore the two older girls with tortured hair and shiny lip gloss at the other end of the bar, whispering to each other and smiling at me. I nodded to Buddy, the cadaverous bartender, who shuffled over, a cigarette clinging to his bottom lip as if attached with a drop of Krazy Glue.

"You know those things'll kill you," I said.

"We're all killing ourselves one way or another, and we all succeed in the end. Whad'ya need, Quinn?"

Buddy never ever smiled but he always cracked me up. "Another Bud, a shot of Cuervo, and a pack of Camel Unfiltered," I said with a grin.

He handed them over. Without thinking, I picked up the sweaty beer bottle with my bad hand. My wrist buckled a bit, and I braced it with the other one. I put the bottle down on the bar and quickly strapped the air cast back around my wrist.

"Y'arright?" croaked Buddy.

"Yeah, yeah, it's nothing."

Buddy glanced down at the lip gloss girls, then back to me, raising his eyebrows in a silent question.

"Not interested," I said. Not today.

"Mmmhmm" he said, sliding his gray bar towel down the countertop.

I pulled my pearl-handled pocketknife out of my knapsack with my good hand and opened it with a clean snap. In a move I'd practiced so much I could do it like breathing, I sliced open the top of the Camels, flipped a cig into my mouth with the point of the knife, then twirled the open knife backward around my middle finger before snapping it closed. Super slick. I slipped it back in my knapsack with my notebook and the bag of meat, and slung the whole thing back onto the sticky floor at the foot of my barstool.

The drunk hipster girl slid onto the barstool next to me. Even without looking directly at her, I formed a quick opinion: the gap between her front teeth was kind of cool and ballsy, but she'd be prettier without the ill-advised jet-black dye job.

"Three bull's-eyes," she said to the air, then turned and focused her gaze on the side of my face as I studied my shot of tequila. "We just won that game with three bull's-eyes—did you see? I mean, I wasn't the one who got them, but I totally held up my end of the team. And I'm so totally messed up, too." I downed the shot and clunked the glass back on the bar. I could feel it spider-webbing through my veins, warm and tingly. I spun away from the bar and headed toward the pool table, catching a glimpse of the hipster girl's black bra strap and pale shoulder, poking out of her too-big plaid shirt.

As I walked away, I heard Hipster Bra-Strap say to Buddy, "Two more tequilas, Maestro."

I racked up a triangle of pool balls and rested the cue on the back of my air cast to break them, sinking a few. As I circled the table, putting balls away, I backed into the space of the Bull's-Eye-Making Punk Rock Girl, who was still playing darts with the bikers.

"Excuse you," she said, ice cold.

I turned to get a good look at her. Under the fierce makeup, she was actually really cute. "Can I just get this shot?" I asked.

"I don't know. Can you?"

"Not if you're in my space."

She held up a dart, with its feathery green party in the back and sharp, shiny business in the front. "I think the metal spike gets priority over the blunt wooden stick. I could poke your eye out with this." A live wire, this girl.

I twirled my pool cue. "Well...I could bash you over the head with this."

"I said, 'I could poke your eye out,'" she insisted.

"Well, I could skewer you and roast you over hot coals."

She frowned. "I'm not playing some kind of S and M 'rock paper scissors' here. I'm serious. Do you want me to poke your stupid eye out or are you gonna move?"

Finally realizing she wasn't flirting, I backed away and let her take her turn. She hit another bull's-eye and didn't so much as glance back at me. I noticed the water bottle in her off hand. Who came to a bar and just drank water? Maybe she wasn't old enough, though, with the makeup it was hard to tell. I just couldn't figure out her deal.

I turned back to the pool table and started lining up my shot again. Hipster Bra-Strap found me again, tottering over from the bar with two sloshing shot glasses.

"I don't think you're nearly messed up enough." She held out a tequila shot toward me. "My treat."

I didn't take it. Too easy, and not interesting. Besides, I had things I needed to hurry up and not think about. I didn't want to go home—I just wanted to hide out here and drink and play pool and take a break from everything. But this girl wasn't going away. She put the shot glasses down on the pool table blocking my angle, and stepped in close enough that I could smell the combination of sweat, tequila, and girly deodorant radiating off of her. She nabbed the cigarette out of my hand and took a long drag.

I nodded over at the Water-Drinking Punk Rock Darts Girl. "Nice girl, your friend."

"She's not my friend—I just met her half an hour ago. Haven't I seen you before? Did you ever work at that Burger King over by the high school?

"No."

"You go to school here?"

"For a while."

"I knew it! What year?"

"Didn't graduate."

"Who'd you hang out with?"

I shrugged.

"You look so familiar. My name's Sydney—ring a bell? Yes? No?"

She was getting irritated with me.

"Well, who the hell are you, what's your name? Come on, Mysterioso, give me a hint."

Ahh, I didn't really want to go here, did I? I plucked my cigarette from her mouth and took a drag off of it, the ash flaring red. She stared at me, expectantly.

Then, looking her straight in the eye, I slowly, deliberately, stubbed the cigarette out on the pale inside plane of my left forearm. It sizzled faintly.

She yelped and scrambled away from me, spilling the drink she was holding across the shamrock felt of the pool table.

"Awww, now you've wasted a shot of perfectly good tequila."

Sydney stared at me for a moment, then turned and shouted over to the bikers, "Did you see that? Check this guy out!"

The constellation of people in the bar shifted, with people moving either closer to or away from me—except for one person. I glanced over and noticed that Punk Rock Darts Girl was simply standing there, observing me with a strangely neutral expression on her face. Then she turned, threw on her zipper-y leather jacket and left the bar.

"So, what's the trick?" asked Sydney.

"No trick," I said.

She seemed confused for a moment, then her eyes sparked with recognition and she smiled. "You're sick."

She reached over and slowly ran her fingers along the burnt, blistering spot on my arm. "Your name is Quill, or Quid or something, right?" I nodded. "Yeah, I remember, you were always getting into fights and shit. I think you knew my friend Dara…red hair, pretty cute…nice rack."

"Oh, yeah…sure." I had zero recollection. But, you know, if I had to be honest, there were a lot of girls I didn't really remember.

Sydney ran her fingers flirtatiously over the scars on my arm, tracing around the small tattooed Bat symbol on the inside of my wrist.

"She told me about you. She thought you were cool…"

I don't know how to explain it, except to say that the tequila had melted my mind slightly. My determination to forget the first part of the day had hit a roadblock. A roadblock with a black bra strap. So I gave my mind permission to flow down another path.

I turned to Buddy. "Two more Cuervos, please." Buddy complied. He'd seen it happen this way before.

There would be more shots, more pool, a scouting mission out into the streets to procure floppy paper plates of pizza. There would be another bar, more beers, some blotto stumbling down the sidewalk, shoulders pressed together for support. Some singing of made-up lyrics and a detour into an alley so I could take a piss against a brick wall. Her head resting on my back as I did, asking if she could hold it. It was too late for that, I'd say, zipping up, but she thought maybe it wasn't, if I knew what she meant. There would be kissing, sloppy and urgent.

There would be more than one way to forget.

13. Quinn

THE SECOND THING PEOPLE always ask me—after pinching my arm and saying "does this hurt?"—is "uh, so...what does sex feel like?" Uh...*seriously*? Did you really just ask me that? People think because I can't feel pain that maybe I don't feel that. Well, I don't have anything to compare it to, but its fine, okay? Let's not talk about it any more. Though, I guess I do have to talk about it just a little bit, because something weird happened that night.

I don't even totally remember how we got back to my house—let's just say I have an incomplete slideshow of images—but we must've managed to stagger into the house and down the stairs to my room because all of a sudden there we were with not very many clothes on, some loud fucking rawk on, so loud you weren't even in your own head anymore, you were in the music's head. That's one good thing about living down in the basement—I can play it loud.

I do remember that, as my body got busy fooling around, my mind kept flashing back to that neutral expression the Darts-Playing Girl had on her face when I put the cigarette out on my arm. I've found that there are usually two kinds of girls—the ones who are into me because oh they think I'm all weird and dark and effed up, and the ones who just think I'm a jerk and want nothing to do with me. It's always one or the other, and I've always thought that's because I'm kind of not that good at reading people, and I don't really show a lot of emotions about stuff or care whether people like me or whatever, so I guess I come across as kind of an ass. It's just that some people like that and other people don't—not much I can do about it since it's just how I am.

I think I wasn't always, though—after my mom left us, I guess I was really sad. I mean I was five and my mom was gone, so it's no wonder. It's weird because I don't really remember much about my mom, to be honest, just little flashes here and there—but I do remember how I felt afterward. I felt like a black hole. Apparently, all I wanted to do was bang my head against the floor. I did it so hard that I knocked myself unconscious and they took me to the hospital. Three times. And I remember my dad sitting me down on one of the aqua plastic chairs in our kitchen not long after that, and telling me I needed to be tough on the inside, and I remember deciding right at that moment that I would do it. Maybe I thought it might make him like me better, or that at least if I was tough that it would protect me against anything ever making me feel that bad again. So I just became that way. And one side effect of that decision was that when I got older, some girls thought I was an asshole, and others wanted to come home with me.

But I didn't really know what to do with someone like the Darts-Playing Girl who didn't seem to be in either camp. So I tried to stop thinking about her and just focus my fuzzy brain on the girl who was right in front of me.

Sydney scraped her fingernails down my arm, tracing around the fresh cigarette burn. She glanced up at me for a reaction, and then, not seeing one, did it again, harder.

"You like that?" she asked.

"Don't talk."

I figured she might be all into the pain thing. I grabbed her hair and turned her head to the side and bit that exposed tendon-y part of her neck. Not drawing blood or anything, but kinda hard. She seemed a little surprised, but didn't pull away.

And then, just for a split second, I saw a flicker. She suddenly looked like a graphic novel version of herself, slightly crazed and distorted and ultra sexy. At first, I thought maybe I was just thinking of a new character I could draw, so I ignored it—it was late, we were wasted and impatient to get each other's clothes off. But it kept happening. As we got more and more into it, these little flashes kept getting longer and more frequent. I might have even gotten the two versions mixed up at one point and think I grabbed the real Sydney too hard because she kind of yelped—but I only realized that later. At the time, I didn't put the pieces together too well.

So by this point, we were tangled in the sheets, arms and legs wrapping and grabbing and pressing into and against each other, when the room started to warp and spin. I'd never really gotten sick from drinking, and I thought, *whoa, maybe that's what's happening here*—and that was when I saw it.

In the corner of the room. The Black Dog, snarling. I swear it.

I whipped my head around to see it, but it was gone.

"What?" she asked.

"Nothing."

I shook it off. *Cuervo, man.*

She put her hand on my face. "Take it easy, okay?"

Did I mention I'm not even supposed to drink? I mean, more than your average seventeen-year-old is not supposed to drink? For some reason, because of my condition, it affects me like double. So I wasn't *that* surprised that weird things were happening. Yet.

We carried on, and again, just as we got hot and heavy, the room started to turn. And again, I saw something. Except this time it wasn't only the dog. It was also two glowing red eyes. The Demon Boy. He shimmered a little, like he was made out of fluid pencil lines and paint, like he had stepped right out of my drawings.

Fucking A. I jumped out of bed and shakily lit a cig. I stared at the corner of the room—and of course there was no dog and no Demon Boy. Ridiculous.

"Jesus, what's going on?" she asked. Oh right—there was a girl in my bed.

I flipped on my desk light and paced around, trying to make it make sense. I saw Sydney looking around at my room—bare brick, plumbing pipes running along the ceiling, a million sketches stacked on my desk and taped to the walls. Stacks of books and my mom's old vinyl collection. Newspaper taped over the high narrow windows. It's a basement. The sweet ones immediately start telling me what they would do to redecorate it. The meaner ones just hate on it.

"Really awesome place." She couldn't have sounded more sarcastic if she'd tried.

I tuned her out and sat down at my desk, where I had a piece of plywood propped up at an angle, a makeshift drafting table.

"What are you doing?"

'What does it look like?"

"Uh…is that it? Because I didn't think we were quite done…"

It slow-motion registered in my brain first that she thought I was being rude, and, second, that probably this whole thing hadn't been the best decision in the first place, but then brushed all that aside because this now felt like a matter of life and death. I grabbed my favorite inking pen.

"I have to draw…it's the only way to get things out of my head."

I tried to get some quick images down on paper, but the stupid air cast on my wrist was making it impossible. I ripped it off, tossed it in the corner and tried to draw without it, but my wrist was so puffy and weak that I couldn't make the pencil do what I wanted it to do.

"Shit." I threw the pencil and it disappeared behind a pile of dirty laundry. I pulled some completed drawings out of a drawer, not caring that she might see them. Some people freaked out when they saw them—they were spooky and dark. My favorite artist is this guy Francis Bacon who I found in a book Ms. Barnett, my whackadoodle eighth grade art teacher, lent me that I never returned. Man, *that* dude was dark. I like to think that if Bacon had been born years later, he might've drawn graphic novels, and they would look a little like mine. But I didn't feel like stopping to give an art history lesson to some drunk girl at that moment.

"What are you doing? Can I see?"

"When I'm done."

She settled back into the sheets and cocked her head at me. "I'm kind of flattered. I don't think I ever inspired anyone before."

I didn't bother to correct her. I pulled out some scissors and started attacking my drawings.

✹

I lost track of time. Sydney quickly lost interest and fell asleep. Since I couldn't draw, I was cutting up old drawings and piecing them together in new, collaged panels—it was a crude way to do it, but I had to do something. The images were like aliens in my body that I had to pull out before they ate me from the inside.

I was working on this panel of the Demon Boy, who was running and looking over his shoulder. I took a cut-out of the black dog and glue-sticked it in so the dog was now chasing the Demon. It wasn't quite in the right place, so I peeled it up, reangled it onto the page, and pressed it down again. Suddenly, the dog really looked like it was scrambling to catch the Demon Boy, who was grinning evilly as he slipped into the shadows.

Then—*BAM!*—the drawing just exploded off the page, filling the room around me. It was like I'd just stepped into the world I had drawn. Hallucinogenic, chaotic, disorienting. I could only catch glimpses of the dog and the Demon Boy as I tried to get my bearings. I heard a spatter of footsteps behind me and spun around just in time to see the Demon snarl and throw a fireball straight toward me so I ducked—

And as quick as it had come on, it was gone. Just me, crouching in my dark room, gasping to catch my breath, while a girl snored obliviously in my bed. I didn't know what had just happened, but I hoped to hell it was a result of too much to drink, because it wasn't something I ever wanted to repeat.

I gathered up the offending drawings and put them in the bathroom sink. I lit a cigarette and, with the same match, lit the drawings on fire. My hands shook as I smoked and watched the pages dematerialize into smoke and ash.

14. Punk Rock Darts Girl

THE T SCREECHED, BRAKING as it approached my stop.

I glanced at the old woman sleeping across the seats on the other side of the subway car from me. Her eyes were hidden by her parka hood, but I could see her toothless mouth moving, like she was chewing gum in her sleep. Some shopping bags stuffed with dirty-looking clothes and blankets sat on the subway floor in front of her. I wondered if the conductor would wake her at the end of the line, or if she could go back and forth until everything shut down for the night. I thought I should leave her something—a bottle of water, a dollar, something, and dug through the pockets of my leather jacket to see what I had, but I had no cash at all and just a linty piece of gum. Then I reasoned that leaving a homeless person a bottle of water was not enough to really have any impact anyway, and that the thing to do would be to invite her home with me and give her a place to stay, but that would probably backfire, because really what you had to do was fix the mental illness or alcohol problem or whatever was causing them to be homeless in the first place, and, besides, its not like my dad would put up with me inviting smelly old women to stay on our couch for one hot minute anyway.

As I stared at the woman, *faith without works* is what kept running through my head, *faith without works*, but as usual I was too indecisive, too overwhelmed to turn feelings into actions. And I hated that.

A group of boys at the far end were the only other people in the subway car, and they were being loud and rowdy, elbowing each other in a way that felt like a joke could transform into a fight without warning. They were probably only sixteen or seventeen, but they were snarly and rude and I couldn't wait to slip out the doors as soon as the car came to a stop.

One of the boys spun away from the friend who was play-boxing him and slid down the bench toward the old woman, bumping into her feet. She didn't wake up but then he bumped her again, this time on purpose, trying to make his idiot friends laugh.

The train came to rest and the doors slid open. It was my stop, and I reflexively stood up, but as the doors lingered open, with the conductor announcing the station through tinny fuzzy speakers, I hesitated. I didn't want to leave this woman sleeping alone with these guys. The boy sitting by the woman's feet, track-suited with a sharp-edged five-o'clock-shadow, turned and looked me square in the eyes without smiling. He glanced down at my clothes, my Doc Marten tough-girl boots, then curled up the side of his mouth, and I braced myself for an insult or a gross comment—reminding myself that I was dressed to fight fire with fire—but before he could speak, the rest of his herd suddenly noticed where we were, and jostled and pushed each other, including the guy across from me, out the door. I remained on the train as the doors closed and we lurched out of the station.

I stayed with the sleeping woman until she woke up and got off a couple of stops later. I got off, too. I watched her shuffle through the empty station with her bags and thought about following as she hobbled up the stairs and out to the street, thought of offering to buy her some dinner, but I didn't. I did nothing. I just jigged down the stairs to the other platform, got on the train heading in the opposite direction and went home.

✖

IN MY ROOM, I stared into the full-length mirror and wiped an oiled cotton ball over one eye, smearing charcoal black across my cheek. *Key Largo* was playing on the clunky old portable TV on the dresser that I kept permanently tuned to the local station that played black and white movies all night.

This half-dressed, half-made up person. One combat boot kicked off on the floor, half punk, half I don't know what. I think I wore these clothes tonight to get a break from feeling overwhelmed, a break from being afraid to take up space, being afraid to act, but it didn't work that well. I'd gone out to play darts, to be around no one I knew because I needed to get out of my house and out of my head, but that guy with the cigarette in the bar had ended my evening on an unsettling note. Not like he wasn't attractive—he was, that's what I noticed first—but his party trick or whatever it was of putting it out on his arm? It was repulsive, jerky, dramatic, and manipulative. Clearly he wanted some *ooh*s and *ah*s and I wasn't going to be part of that. But what made me stare, what I found oddly mesmerizing, was his willingness to be a really specific person in the world. To take up space. That was it—he had committed to something. That something might be to being an ass, but at least he'd committed.

I looked in the mirror, one boot on, one boot off, one eye made up, the other bare. There were some decisions I needed to make. One really big one in particular. But I just didn't know how.

15. Caitlin

YELLOW MORNING LIGHT STREAMED into the kitchen, which was full of off-duty firemen, uncomfortably shrugging the shoulders of their suit jackets and bantering over coffee and danishes. Will played host, hunting down more mugs and joking that he never knew where things were kept in this damn place.

Caitlin carried Winnie into the room; the top of Winnie's head nestled shyly in the hollow of her mother's neck as her eyes darted around, taking in the scene. Caitlin nuzzled her hair, which smelled like strawberry shampoo. The men clustered around them warmly, hugging Caitlin and marveling over how big Winnie had gotten. It felt like a family reunion.

Even though she knew the guys from the force would turn out, it was still a bit of a shock to see so many of them in their house like this. In a way, they were her father's real family. There was no one else coming to town—her aunt Dorothy, her father's only sister, was agoraphobic and wouldn't travel from Philadelphia. With no one to wait for, she'd scheduled a simple service for today to get it over with as soon as possible. She found viewings and open caskets gruesome, and he'd been so sick for so long, it had all felt like one big lead-up to the funeral. Why wait longer? Plus this was her day off anyway, and it was probably best not to ask for more time off at work.

An older, tanned, and craggy-looking fireman with silvery hair kissed Caitlin on the cheek and slipped a fat envelope into her hand.

"It's not much, but we wanted to help," he rasped.

"Oh, Richie, no, we can't…"

"Take it, Caity. It's the least we could do for your dad."

Eyes welling up a little, she stopped protesting and took the envelope. She hugged Richie, who smelled like salt air, then cleared her throat, taking a step back to speak to the room.

"Thanks, you guys. I thank you, Will thanks you, and my dad… Well, he probably wouldn't thank you—" They all laughed. "—but I thank you on his behalf…"

As she talked, she half-heard the basement door open at the back of the room behind her, but didn't even look, figuring it was Quinn coming up for coffee. But when a ripple of reactions slowly rolled across the room, all smirks and swiveling heads, she finally turned around to see what was so distracting. A girl she'd never seen before, with smeared makeup and serious bedhead, was standing at the counter, quietly helping herself to some coffee and fruit. The distracting part was what she was wearing—just boxer shorts and a torn tank top that didn't leave much to the imagination.

"Oh, hey," the girl said, holding up a pastry, "Is it a problem if I snag the last apple thing?"

16. Quinn

I WAS SLUMPED AT THE drawing table, where I'd been all night, smoking and staring at a blank sheet of paper.

Sydney came downstairs with a plate of food. "What's with the lumberjack convention?" she asked, all sunny, popping a grape into her mouth.

"What?"

"In your kitchen. Lots of large men in cheap suits."

"They're firemen."

She peered over my shoulder at the blank sheet of paper on the desk.

"Guess you *weren't* that inspired."

I didn't want to get into it. I just got up and pulled the first aid kit out from under the bed, grabbed some ointment and a gauze bandage.

"So what are they doing here?" she pressed.

"Friends of the family. My sister's husband is a fireman. My dad was a fireman."

She sat down next to me on the bed, real close, and ran her finger up and down my arm with the cigarette burn, purring.

"So I guess putting out fires is genetic?"

I reclaimed my arm, dabbed some ointment on the burn and started wrapping the bandage around it.

"They're here on account of my dad died."

"What? When?"

"Yesterday."

She was silent for a moment as she tried to reconcile this information. When she spoke again, her breath was uneven, her voice a little higher.

"Your dad. The fireman. He died."

"Yeah. I guess if they're wearing suits the funeral's probably today."

"So last night while we were at the bar…and while we were…*fucking*, your dad had just…?"

I shrugged.

"What is your *problem*?" she screeched.

"I don't have a problem. You do, apparently."

I mean, I felt sorta bad that she felt bad—but I wasn't sure what I should have done differently. Was I supposed to have sat her down before we'd kissed and said "hey, I totally want to take your clothes off right now, but I just wanted to tell you that my dad died twelve hours ago. Now, let's get to it!"? I mean, come on.

She scooped up her things, her purse, her bra, her pants. "I think…I gotta go."

I nodded, finishing up my bandaging job, "I kinda figured."

17. Caitlin

As CAITLIN MADE HERSELF busy fixing a fresh pot of coffee, she spoke to Will under the hum of conversation in the room, trying not to sound as brittle as she felt. "This is as difficult for him as it is for any of us. He's just coping in his own way." He wasn't buying it and she wasn't even sure she believed herself.

Sydney came stomping up the stairs and through the kitchen, still fastening her bra under her shirt, and stormed out the back door without saying a word to anyone. The firemen pretended not to notice, but Caitlin was mortified.

Will nodded. "I'm coping, too—so would it be okay with you if I brought home a different girl every night?"

"I think it's just a phase."

"It's not a phase, it's a fucking way of life."

Caitlin winced—"The F-word..."—and nodded to Winnie, who was over at the food table, systematically poking her finger into each pastry, trying to find out what flavors were inside.

Caitlin caught a whiff of something bad and made a face. "Do you smell something?"

Winnie held up a drippy jelly donut. "Mommy, can I have another?"

"No, honey, you had enough."

Will was not dropping it. "How long can you keep making excuses for him? He's only getting worse."

"I know."

"It's making you nuts, it's making me nuts."

"I know. Things are going to change."

"How many times have I heard that? I think I've been really patient, I gotta be honest with you. But now your dad is gone and it's time to deal with this."

"Mommy, I'm still hungry!" howled Winnie.

"Half, you can have a half." Caitlin turned, fed-up to Will. *Today of all days.* "Look, I don't know what to do about it, I don't know what to do about *him.*"

"We talked about it."

"I don't know. Let's just wait and see."

"How long do we wait?"

Winnie, below the grown-ups' radar, bent down and took Quinn's pearl-handled knife out of his knapsack, which lay, forgotten, under the kitchen table. She used it, precariously, to cut her doughnut in half, then tried to close the knife by flipping it over her hand like Quinn. Not really coordinated enough to do it, but she kept trying. Flip, clatter. Flip, flip, clatter. No one noticed her.

The firemen were getting restless. Richie checked his watch and stepped nearer to Caitlin. "Caity, we should probably start heading over soon."

Flip, clatter. "Mommy!" Winnie exploded into tears, blood dripping from a cut on her hand.

Caitlin rushed to her, practically skidding under the table on her knees and scooping her up "Jesus, what happened? What did you do?" She examined Winnie's hand—thankfully superficial. Seeping, not gushing.

Will picked the knife up off the linoleum, folded it and put it in his pocket. He peeled Winnie off of Caitlin and carried her upstairs. "Let's go put a Band-Aid on it, make it all better. I told you we don't play with knives."

"Uncle Quinn does that," Winnie managed to get out, between sobs.

Will called back over his shoulder, "Great thing to teach a four-year-old, Cait. Like you said, things are going to change— and they're going to change now."

Caitlin nodded. She turned to the concerned firemen. "Go, you guys, we'll meet you there."

They slowly started filing out the back door. Caitlin slumped into a chair. Maybe Will was right. Maybe it was time. There was that disgusting smell again. Looking around, she saw Quinn's knapsack under the table, partly unzipped. She pulled the flap open all the way and the stink wafted out. She extracted the mushy bag of meat that must have been sitting in there overnight and pitched it into the trash.

Quinn wandered up the stairs. The cast was back on his wrist, and the cigarette burn was bandaged. He nodded to the last of the firemen headed out the door and patted Caitlin on the back as he opened the fridge to window shop.

"Hey. What's up?" he said, casual as a T-shirt.

"Go get dressed. You're coming to the service," she snapped.

"Since when do you tell me what to do?"

"Do it."

He stared at her like her words were little burning nuggets of coal she had dropped in his bare hands.

Richie, the tough-looking fireman, was the last one out the door. He caught Quinn's eye with a stern gaze, like he was trying to will him to get his act together just this once, for his dad's sake. Or maybe he was just glad the old man wasn't here to see this.

18. Quinn

I PUT ON A BUTTON-UP shirt—the only decent one I had—but couldn't find my one tie, and, honestly, didn't really look that hard. Caitlin noticed, of course, but didn't say anything. It was only ten o'clock by the time we all piled into the car, and she already looked exhausted. Me and Winnie sat in the backseat, like we were both Cait and Will's kids or something. What a messed-up joke.

As we pulled away from the house, I saw a small, forgotten, yellow dump truck in the middle of the empty schoolyard across the street. It was Saturday, and the asphalt plain felt mysterious and naked without any kids. If you saw it in a horror movie, you would hear the spooky creak of one of the empty swings swaying in the breeze.

✺

I WAS SIX YEARS old in that same schoolyard, playing, when another kid bashed his big metal truck into mine.

"Stop it!"

He crashed it into my leg.

"I said stop it."

The kid kept hitting me with it, watching me for a reaction. I knew what he was doing and tried to ignore it, but it finally got so annoying I grabbed the truck from his hand and hit him across the face with it, hard. He burst into big, sloppy sobs and the other kids gathered around, pushing in on me. It was too much and I swung the truck around trying to clear a circle around myself. I might have swiped some other kids with it, I don't know, but more kids started crying anyway and the teachers ran over, talking slow and quiet. First, I thought they were talking to the crying kids, but then realized they were talking to me, like I was a dangerous animal.

"Put the truck down, Quinn... Call his father."

I backed away from them, confused—I hadn't started it, I just wanted them to leave me alone. I threw the truck at the teachers as hard as I could and ran in the other direction, climbing to the top of the igloo-shaped climbing structure. Leave me alone. *But the teachers followed and the other kids did, too, standing cowardly in the teachers' long shadows.*

"Weirdo!"

"Stupid freak!"

The teachers tried to herd them away. I stood up on top of the igloo, much taller than even the teachers, I listened to them shouting names at me, and I smiled. That was when I realized how to keep them away.

✖

"I SAID, 'YOU'RE WEARING a clean shirt, aren't you?'"

I had the same small smile on my face now, staring out the car window.

"Quinn, is that a clean shirt?"

"What? Yeah."

That didn't mean there hadn't been fights. I was in a fight almost every week with some kid who thought they could "make me feel it." Somehow I'd gotten out of that schoolyard alive. My strategy had helped me make it this far. Survival had always been the goal. But I was starting to wonder what for?

✶

BECAUSE I HAD BARELY slept the night before, I nodded off during the service for my dad. When I woke up, slouched in my folding chair, the box was already in the ground. To say that Caitlin was ticked off would be the understatement of the year.

✶

WHEN I SAW CAIT and Will giving each other silent-but-meaningful looks across the front seat during the drive home, I thought it was just them being all tightly wound about the funeral. But when we got off the highway at an unfamiliar exit, I knew something else was up.

We pulled up in front of a large house in a weird part of the city. The little sign next to the door said "FamilyCare Residential Center."

"What the hell is this?" I asked.

Will said, "We're taking a little tour. Let's go."

Winnie clambered out of her booster seat and went along with Will and Caitlin—who wouldn't look me in the eye—up to the porch of the house. I stayed in the car. Seriously, what the hell? Some social worker-type lady in a smocky shirt came out to greet them. Sitting on the porch were some of the so-called "residents." Residents, prisoners—tomato, tomah-to. Two glassy-eyed, librarian-sweatered women chain-smoked and played a card game. Winnie climbed up on a bench and sat next to a slow-moving guy working on a coloring book. Come on, this was too much. I got out of the car, shouting.

"I am *not* living here with these freakin' junkies and 'challenged' whatevers. I'd rather die."

Caitlin and Will hurried back toward me. I knew I was embarrassing Cait; that was 100 percent my point.

"Quinn, shhhh…"

"You can't just send me here, I'm almost eighteen."

Will stepped in, all macho-man-in-charge. "This may be news to you, but if you're a danger to yourself, or to others, you will absolutely be put somewhere where people can keep an eye on you twenty-four hours a day."

"And who decides if I'm a danger—you?"

Now Caitlin with her calmy-calm voice, though she couldn't even look at me. "A psychiatrist has to do an evaluation."

"You know an awful lot about how this works."

"It's an option we're seriously considering," said Will.

"'An option we're seriously considering'? What is this, power windows on your new car? Fuck you."

"Do you see what you're doing to your sister?"

Cait put a hand on his arm. "Will, stop."

"It's the best thing for this family. Our family," said Will.

I rolled my eyes. I mean, my dad had been dead for what, a day, and he was pulling this "our family" stuff?

"Don't you get it? Don't you get how hard it is for everyone because of you?" he snarled.

"Yeah, life's a big awesome party for me, too."

Furious, Will took a step closer to me and put his face right in my face.

Caitlin was freaking. "Don't, you'll hurt him!"

Will looked like he might burst a vein in his muscly neck. As he talked, I watched the little spit drops spew. It was like my brain was shutting down and I was watching the movie version of my life.

"You're useless! You sit around all day, doing nothing, contributing nothing, screwing everyone else's lives up—yeah I feel real sorry for you."

"It's not his fault..." Caitlin interjected.

"Of *course* it is!"

And when he glanced away to yell at Caitlin, I jumped him, swinging wildly. He weighs like twice as much as me, so that probably wasn't the smartest thing, but my body just was on autopilot. I got one good punch in before Caitlin pulled me off him.

"Stop it!"

"Jesus!" roared Will, rubbing his ear.

Caitlin turned to him, "Can you just leave us alone for a second?" He reluctantly went up onto the porch to sit with Winnie, who was starting to bawl for some unarticulated reason.

"What the hell do you want from me?" I asked Cait.

"I just want you to live like a normal human being."

"I'm not a normal human being."

"Cut it out, Quinn. Jesus...I just... I don't know what else to do. I can't keep doing this, the way things have been. And I know things have been really stressful with Dad and everything, but you've been pushing me and pushing me—and I'm losing it. I'm seriously losing my mind, seeing what you do to yourself. I feel responsible."

I noticed that the bandage that had been covering my new burn was starting to slip down my arm and show below the cuff of my shirt—I shoved my hand into my jacket pocket so she wouldn't see.

"You're not responsible," I said.

"But I am. I will be responsible for you for the rest of your life—" she cracked a smile, trying to lighten things up, "—whether you like it or not."

I had to salvage this thing. Had to get her to back off until I could come up with a plan. "Give me a little time, Cait. Things will change, I promise."

"Things just… They can't be the way they've been."

"Just give me a couple of weeks—if things aren't better for you, I'll come make pattycakes with 'Special Ed' over there."

It was supposed to be a joke, but it made her burst into tears. Will came back over, carrying Winnie.

"What's going on? What did you say to your sister?"

She put a hand on his chest, reflexively keeping him away from me. "He wants a chance. For things to change."

"Right… And how would they change?"

"Well, there would have to be no more 'accidents,' right?" She looked to me and I nodded.

"How about getting some kind of job?" he said, looking me in the eye.

Caitlin shifted her weight, uneasy. "You know how I feel about that."

"You can't protect him from everything."

"What am I gonna do, anyway? I have no qualifications, no diploma…"

"Well, maybe if someone had made you finish school—" Will caught himself. Changed his tone. "There *is* an opening at the fire station."

"Ha ha, very funny."

"Working the phones." He turned to Caitlin. "I'm only trying to be helpful, to find another option, but forget it, I don't care, leave him here."

"Just quit it, quit it you two," she snapped. She paced around in a small circle between us, rubbing her face with indecision so hard I thought her skin might come off.

"He's coming home," she finally declared to Will. I thought I'd won that round—until she turned to me with the kicker, "*But* you have to take care of yourself, and have to get a job—a *safe* job. Otherwise, this is your home. It's your choice."

Yeah, I did have a choice, and at that moment, I suddenly understood what it was. And it sure wasn't either of the ones she had given me.

19. Quinn

I T WASN'T MY DAD dying that affected me. I'm sure it sounds bad, but I swear that's the truth, I really didn't care. But the one-two punch of not being able to draw, and now this bullshit that Will was forcing Caitlin to do, made me feel like I was sitting in a rowboat and someone had just tossed my two tether ropes off the dock. Unmoored. That was the word that kept popping up in my mind. Unmoored.

I sat in the aqua chairs at the kitchen table with Caitlin the next morning. She was surfing through some job listings on her ancient laptop and I was supposed to be circling some in the newspaper, but all I was doing was trying to draw my characters over the top of the classifieds with my left hand—to see if I could. I couldn't really.

"Here you go—'file clerk, will train.'" She sounded overly perky. I wanted to flick my pen at her.

"Awesome, Cait."

"I know it's not the most exciting thing, but we have to find you a job."

"Ooh, I could get a paper cut. I could staple myself."

"Ha ha." She was determined to ignore my sullen cloud. "This is going to work. I have a good feeling."

"Yeah…"

"I think you should just go to these places in person, it's better than calling. Way better than emailing."

She went back to the computer screen, and I went back to my drawings. They were like medical illustrations done by an eight-year old of various mortal wounds. It was that kind of a morning. I guess I'm the kind of person who, if I'm gonna kill myself, I want to try to draw it first. I knew it was the best thing for everyone, and it didn't scare me at all. It seemed like a rational decision, maybe the first one I had ever made.

✖

I LEFT THE HOUSE with Caitlin's detailed list of job leads—and tossed it into the first trash can I saw. I had other business to take care of.

✖

"YOU GOT SOMETHING TO show me, dickweed?" Steve had amped up his usual greeting. He was really wound up.

"Not yet, assclown, but I will soon. I know the ending now."

"What is it?"

"You'll see."

"Come on, man, I think I can still call that guy and convince him to look at your stuff—just give me something I can run with."

"What's going on, why are you so edgy? Did you have to borrow money from Miranda again this month?" Steve's girlfriend was always on him to make more money, to at least have the store break even, which I'm not sure it ever had, and it stressed him out.

"No. I mean, yeah, I did, just a little. But listen, man..." He got all serious. "I want to send it because it's just...good. Really fucking good."

I was kind of shocked by the earnestness of his compliment. We never talked like that and I didn't know how to respond. So I didn't. I just opened my backpack and pulled out a stack of comics I knew he'd flip for. Real collectables.

"I just came by to give you these." I handed them over and he fanned through the pristine plastic sleeves, stunned.

"Original *Sandman*? Jesus, man, these are mint. What's going on? You going somewhere? You better not go anywhere without getting *your* book to me."

"Don't worry, I'll finish it. I'll get it to you."

"Where are you going?"

I didn't want the twenty questions, so I was already out the door. "Catch you later."

He yelled after me, "Draw, asshole! What else are you good for?!"

✖

I just walked. I guess this was the upside of "unmoored."

Down the street, I saw a girl frantically searching for something, looking inside dumpsters, down narrow alleys. She was oddly dressed—like a character from a 1940s movie or something—with crisp ironed pants and a silky ivory blouse under a bright white apron. Her hair was down and wavy in that super-precise 1940s way that I didn't even know how anyone knew how to do anymore, and she had perfect red lipstick and movie-star makeup that was streaked by tears. She carried something under her arm.

"Tommy, Tommy, where are you?" she cried.

I didn't know who Tommy was, but he must've been pretty small if he was hiding inside garbage cans. As I passed by her on the sidewalk, I almost did a double take when I got close enough to see her face.

"Hey, you're…"

I didn't know her name, but it was definitely that girl from the bar—the cute punk-rock girl with the killer darts. But now she looked totally different, and she was acting differently, too, to match her new clothes. Now she looked like she was my age, maybe even younger. She didn't recognize me.

"Excuse me, but have you seen a fat orange cat with one ear?" she asked me. She knelt down and peered underneath a parked car. "Tommy!"

"Tom the cat? Good name."

"His full name is Tom Jones."

"Like that old singer guy? Do the girl cats throw their underwear at him?"

She stood up and looked at me, hands on her hips. "You know, it's not that I don't appreciate your witty comments, but I'd really prefer it if you'd just help me look for—" The light of recognition clicked on in her eyes. "—oh…you."

Suddenly self-conscious, she dabbed at her sniffly nose with a handkerchief. A handkerchief! She was playing dress-up in a serious way, so I played along.

"I never had a chance to formally introduce myself." I held out my hand. "Quinn."

She shook it tentatively. "Reese."

"I almost didn't recognize you. That outfit—it's, uh… pretty different."

"I woke up this morning feeling very Lauren Bacall."

"Actress?" I asked.

She looked at me like I was a stone cold idiot. I guess the Punk-Rock-Girl persona was still in there somewhere. "Duh. She was in *To Have and Have Not*? *The Big Sleep*?"

"No, I meant *you* are you an actress or something?"

"No."

"Multiple personality disorder?"

She turned to walk away.

"Hey, just kidding. I'm just not sure which one is the real you."

"I don't know what you are talking about. Tom Jones!"

Bursting into tears again, she ran over and pulled a fat and uncooperative orange cat out from behind a dumpster.

"But isn't that him?" I asked, totally confused.

She hugged the grouchy old thing to her chest. "Yes."

"So why are you crying?"

"I don't know. I can't help it." The drops of her tears perched on the surface of the cat's gingery fur, as if he had been waterproofed. "I was trying to put a sign in the window and he slipped out the door… Didn't you, you crazy little man…"

"Mrrrehhhh," griped the cat.

I caught a glimpse of the sign she was carrying under her arm. It said "Help Wanted."

"Are you hiring?"

"Yes, why?" she asked warily.

I pointed at myself.

"What, you're looking for a job?"

"Yeah."

"You don't even know what the job is."

"Doesn't matter."

"It's working in my dad's shop."

"Where?"

She pointed a few doors down, to the butcher shop where I'd gotten Cait's meat the day before. I almost busted out laughing.

"You work there?" I asked, incredulous.

"Yeah. It's my dad's shop."

"Wow..." It was like the funniest cosmic joke ever. "That's so perfect."

"I don't think so."

"Are you kidding? It's ideal for me."

"I *really* don't think so."

"I was actually just looking for a job, and bingo, there you are with 'help wanted' under your arm. Maybe it's like some kind of sign."

"Duh, yeah, it's a sign."

"No, like a sign from, you know, the universe or God or something. If you believe in that kind of thing."

"I actually do. Though I somehow doubt that God has been reduced to writing His will in big red letters on a plastic card."

I shrugged. "It's hard to find stone tablets these days."

✦

I WAITED ALONE IN front of the meat counter for a few minutes. I noticed that the gray rabbit I had seen hanging in the window was gone. The ducks were still there though.

The lunkheaded guy from last time came out and tossed some chicken parts into the case.

"Hey, it's Mister Fresh Ground Beef. You still looking for free dog food?"

I tried hard not to meet sarcasm with sarcasm. "No, that's all taken care of, thanks."

He muttered to himself like people do who aren't smart enough to keep their thoughts contained, "Free bones, yeah right."

He retreated to the back room again and soon Reese and her butcher dad came out. I stood up straight, like a job-seeker, and clasped my hands behind my back casually, to hide the air cast on my right wrist.

"I'm sorry," her dad said from under his shrubby mustache, "we really are looking for someone who has worked in a butcher shop before." He was the owner of the Italian accent I had heard from the back room the day before. Old school.

"Oh, I have, sir," I assured him.

Reese bore into me with her eyes—*really?* I kept my gaze on her dad.

"Oh, well then, Theresa misinformed me. Right now I need someone to help mostly with deliveries and prep work—trimming, grinding, these kind of things."

"Well, if, as they say, every man is an artist in something, then meat is my medium. In fact, I'm never happier than when I have a sharp knife in my hand." Okay, so I got a little carried away. But he bought it.

"Excellent. There you go. You know, I was afraid I wouldn't find anyone for this job, but it seems I'm lucky right out of the bat. It is important that we find someone to replace Theresa so she can leave to study at college in a couple of weeks."

He put a proud arm around Reese's shoulders. She smiled uncomfortably.

"Fantastic, everybody wins!" I over-enthused.

"When could you start?" he asked.

"Tomorrow?"

"Perfect. Come at eight in the morning..." He raised his eyebrows, searching for my name.

"Quinn. Quinn Ballard."

"Nice to meet you, Quinn Ballard. A nice Italian name." He chortled at his own joke. I smiled along.

"Irish, but we're nonpracticing."

"Welcome to Raffallo's." He extended his hand, as round and puffy as a potpie, over the display case to shake mine. I coughed to cover the sound of ripping Velcro, then reached my right hand up to seal the deal—holding the air cast out of view behind my back with my left.

I looked over and smiled at Reese but she just stood there next to her dad, head tilted to one side, frowning at me. Like she wasn't sure how that had happened. Like she wanted to rewind because she must have missed an important line that would explain the whole thing, but just realized her remote was dead.

20. Quinn

CAITLIN WAS OUTSIDE, KICKING at the front door.

I bounded up from the basement, two steps at a time, with a pause at the top step to tamp out my cig on the riser and tuck it out of sight. When people ask me why I'm not more careful with my body, I always think of all the people who smoke. Smoking is self-injury that is invisible today, but kills you tomorrow—a calculation that seemed easy to accept for the billions of smokers in the world—so why couldn't they see that that was how my whole life felt?

Cait kicked at the base of the door again. I could see one irritated eye peering in through the dusty glass pane.

"I'm coming, I'm coming!"

I opened the door and she poured through, pushing past me and heading down the hall to the kitchen, balancing two bags of groceries in one arm and Winnie, wearing a pink velvet princess dress, in the other.

"I think you can get down and walk like a big girl now."

"No."

"Come on, Win, Mommy's head hurts and now you want her arms to fall off, too?"

Just as she made it to the safe harbor of the kitchen, about to deposit Winnie and the bags on the kitchen table, one of the bags burst, spilling groceries onto the floor.

"Shit."

"Shit," mimicked Winnie.

"What did Mommy tell you about that word?"

"Only Mommy can say it?"

"Right." She yelled to me, "Can you come help, please?"

I wandered into the kitchen and started to help pick things up. She handed me a bashed-in pint of ice cream.

"Put this in the freezer."

"Ice cream!" shouted Winnie.

"Not 'til after supper," said Caitlin. But while her back was turned, I slurped up a mushy blob of ice cream that had escaped from the lip of the container. Just as Winnie was about to protest, I held it out and gave her a lick, too, sending her into a giggling fit.

"I think I'm getting another migraine. Winnie, will you run up and get Mommy's medicine? Come on, I'll time you." Caitlin made a big show of looking at her watch, doing the routine just like she used to with me when I was little. "Ready...?"

"Uncle Quinn, count it, count it!" shouted Winnie, jumping up and down.

I set the ice cream carton down on the counter and bent over in my best race-starter's pose. "On your mark...get set...GO!"

Winnie sprinted down the hall and up the stairs in a blur of pink velvet, her skinny arms and legs pumping.

"Someday that trick won't work on her anymore," Cait said, "And that will be a sad, sad day."

I smiled and opened the refrigerator, contemplating the contents, mentally assembling a snack. She bumped me aside so she could put some things inside.

"So how's the job search going?" she asked, as casually as she could.

"You know, I kinda found something."

"That's great. What is it?"

"I don't really want to say. But trust me, its good."

"Come on, tell me! Why not, its not for sure yet?"

From upstairs came Winnie's frantic cry. "Mommy, I don't see it, how much more time?"

"Twenty-three seconds!" Caitlin shouted. She turned to me. "The Advil's probably in the cabinet where she can't reach it."

"She'll find it," I said, trying to deflect the request I knew was coming.

"Will you go help her?" There it was.

"I don't really want to go up there."

"Don't be lazy. Go help her."

✷

I PROCEEDED SLOWLY UP the stairs, my eyes trained on the door at the top, the one to the bathroom, which was half closed. Inside I could see Winnie struggling to climb up onto the counter where the sink faucet was dripping slowly, chronically, *drip, drip…* Just past her, on the far wall of the cramped, avocado-tiled room, was the old claw-footed tub.

Winnie glanced over and saw me coming. "Uncle Quinn, hurry!"

"Hold your horses, hippo-head." I hoped my voice didn't betray how unsettled I felt.

I pushed on the door, stepped warily over the bathroom threshold, and reached over to open the medicine cabinet for Winnie.

She pawed at my arm, "Come on, I gotta break the record!"

A box of tampons fell out of the cabinet into the sink, and a prescription bottle rolled out of it. I examined the label— Dilaudid, prescribed to Dad.

Drip, drip, went the faucet…

"You see what you've done?" a deep voice boomed.

I didn't want to look, but I really didn't have a choice.

"You see?" Dad demanded.

I already knew what I would see—I'd seen it in my head every day since I was five. It was worse to see it in this room though, the room where it happened.

I glanced over at the tub and saw Dad kneeling next to it, younger, robust, and substantial, very much alive. Mom was another matter. Her lifeless body was submerged in the blood-clouded water. Nude. A small paring knife lay in a drizzle of blood on the floor next to the tub, same one that she'd used to casually slice a banana onto my cereal for breakfast in the morning before she'd turned it on herself. Her hand, limply draped over the side of the tub, slowly drip dripping *blood off the tip of her middle finger onto the floor.*

Though my stomach had shrunk into a hard, crumpled walnut, I wasn't really surprised. It was always there. That's why I avoided coming in here whenever possible.

"Hurry, Uncle Quinn!" Winnie jumped around me like a puppy, oblivious.

I saw Dad turn toward me to speak, and I knew what was coming, but that didn't make it any easier.

"This is your fucking fault," he hissed at me, face contorted *with grief and rage. He lashed out with a steel-toed boot, sending the paring knife skittling across the tile. "I'd beat the crap out of you if I thought it would make any difference."*

The detail I always noticed was the way my mother's hair, normally so tightly composed around her face, now floated weightless and free. Like a different person. A different mother. I avoided looking at Dad again, hoping, as I had since that day, that keeping everything tightly coiled inside myself might keep anything else bad from happening.

"Hurry!" shrieked Winnie.

Caitlin came up the stairs. "Winnie, stop screaming, the game's over. I'll get it myself." She saw me standing frozen, staring at the empty tub. "Are you okay?"

"Yeah. Fine."

She reached past me and grabbed the Advil bottle from the medicine cabinet, quickly shook out three and swallowed them.

"Now Mommy's headache's all better!" shouted Winnie.

I shoved Dad's prescription bottle into Caitlin's hand. "I thought you were clean."

"I am," she insisted.

I moved past her, desperate to get out of the bathroom and down the stairs. As I passed her, though, she spotted my bare wrist and grabbed me, pulling up my sleeve.

"Where's your cast?"

"The doc said I could take it off after a day."

"I doubt that."

She then noticed the bandage on my forearm, covering the cigarette burn.

"And what's the deal with this?"

"It's nothing. It's old."

"Quinn!"

"I didn't mean to. It just happened."

"Bullshit. You said…"

Winnie piped up, "Bullshit!"

"What did I tell you?" Caitlin snapped at her.

Winnie started to cry.

Caitlin scooped her up, "Oh, sweetie…"

I saw the opening and bolted down the stairs. "I gotta go, I have stuff to do."

She followed after me, yelling. "Always such a goddamned tough guy. How brave is it when it doesn't even hurt?"

As I jumped down the last two stairs and rounded the bannister in the front hallway, Will came in the front door. I pushed right past him, and he shot me a sour look.

"What?" I growled at him.

Caitlin was still shouting from upstairs, "If you don't cut this shit out—"

I disappeared down the basement stairs to my room.

21. Caitlin

"**Y**OU'LL BE OUT OF here so goddamned fast. And don't say I didn't warn you!" Caitlin appeared at the top of the stairs, holding a crying Winnie and shouting after Quinn—stopping short when she saw Will standing at the bottom of the stairs looking up at her.

He didn't try very hard to keep the exasperated look off his face. "What's going on? This is ridiculous."

"I just…nothing. It's my fault," Caitlin backpedalled. She realized she still had her father's pill bottle in her hand and discreetly slipped it into her pocket.

"Now what did he do?"

"Will, he's trying."

"I don't know how smart this whole idea is. In fact, I'm pretty sure it's a huge mistake. But hey, it's your call."

"Daddy!" blubbed Winnie.

Will headed upstairs, peeling his work clothes off. Winnie squirmed out of Caitlin's arms and followed her dad into the bedroom, unspooling a continuous and semi-intelligible string of words about how she was justgettingmommy'sheadachepills and how mommyyelledsoloud at her. He called back over his shoulder, "What the hell's for diner?" And Winnie echoed it, "Hellsfer dinner!"

Caitlin trudged down the stairs and into the kitchen. How did a simple interaction with Quinn so quickly lead to a fight about something else, everything else? Maybe this new job, whatever it was, would help things settle down.

She spotted the damaged ice cream carton that he had left out, now melting in the middle of a sticky puddle on the counter. She picked it up and flung it into the sink, where it exploded spectacularly, covering everything with messy, chocolate-y goop.

She stared at the mess for a long moment, then started cleaning it up.

22. Reese

E WAS HANDSOME, I'LL give him that. James-Dean-in-*Giant* handsome, even. But I was pretty positive I didn't want him working for my dad. I remembered him from the bar and he seemed weird then, but then he was so excited about this dumb job, and he got hired so quick that I couldn't really stop it. It just seemed like a bad idea. First of all, cute guys are usually sort of socially stunted. Everyone comes to them, so they don't have to actually be nice or polite or interested in what you have to say or anything. And cute plus weird *definitely* equaled trouble—though he was cute enough to make me slightly curious what *brand* of weird he was, whether it was the good or bad kind of trouble... And second—

Do you think you can always tell when a wig is a wig? I guess how could you know, because you don't know when it's so convincing that you don't know, right? I had scored big time at a thrift store over Central Square, with some glam silver platform boots that I was envisioning as the centerpiece of a *Runaways*-era Joan Jett ensemble, but I didn't want to cut my hair, so I was considering a wig, but I hate when they look totally fake. Plus, the really good wigs are wicked expensive, as I found out when I tried to get a good Dolly Parton wig last winter when I was totally obsessed with her.

I put the silver platform boots on—they looked stupid with the other recent thrift store score I was wearing—a vintage lace nightgown that I imagined was like the one movie star

Lupe Vélez might have worn in 1944 when she killed herself in spectacular style over a love affair gone wrong, with an overdose of sleeping pills on her bed, surrounded by flowers. (Though, I also read that she'd died with her head in the toilet, throwing up the pills, and was only later placed back on the bed where she had planned to take her last breath... Either way, ultra dramatic, right?) I angled this way and that in the mirror, thinking about Lupe, how she was too sensitive for the world. And about Joan, who was tough and got the world to give her what she wanted. I thought I was definitely more like Lupe and that I needed to summon some more Joan into my life.

It's just, when I start to think too much, which is a lot of the time, I feel overwhelmed. All the animals in the animal shelters that get "put to sleep" every day. The pollution we are pumping into the water and the air and the earth. The innocent people being killed in wars, in famine. The old homeless woman on the subway. It actually makes me feel sick, makes my guts ache like I drank ten cups of black coffee on an empty stomach. I feel like I should start by choosing just one problem to commit to, just one thing to really care about, and do something about—but then I don't. There are too many things that need fixing, and it's paralyzing. So instead I buy a pair of cheap sparkly boots and dress up.

"Theresa?" my dad called out, knocking on my door.

I quickly kicked the boots off into the giant lava flow of clothes on the floor, narrowly missing Tom Jones, who startled out of the heap with a grumpy *mrrrehhhh*.

I opened my door. My dad was standing in the dim hallway, pulling some cash from his beat-up wallet. "Here, I want you to have this, in case you want to buy some things for school. Clothes, books, whatever you need."

"No, Daddy, I'm okay. I have money from work."

"This is extra."

"I'm okay."

He looked a little disappointed. "If you need it, it's here for you."

I nodded, and he turned and shuffled down the hall toward his room, where I knew he would collapse onto the bed fully dressed and be snoring before the local news could even get to the weather report.

I closed my door and pulled out an already-opened envelope from under a pile on my desk. I sat cross-legged on the floor in my Lupe Vélez nightgown and reread the creased letter. The letter that had become a weight around my neck, a heavy, thrilling, confusing, terrifying, crippling weight.

"Dear Theresa Raffallo, We are happy to inform you that you have been selected for admission to Boston University..."

When I first got it, I was so excited. Of course, I immediately told my dad, who was so proud of me—I'd be the first in our family to go to college. And then the worrying began. And the thrift store trips got more intense. And amid all the family excitement, they never realized that I never wrote back to accept. I ignored the follow-up emails. I didn't find out what the financial aid possibilities were, which I definitely would have had to do. I just didn't do anything. My dad always had me deal with school forms and bills and things because even though his English had gotten better over the years, he was still nervous about official stuff—so after he asked me a couple of times if I needed anything from him and I said no, he must've just figured I had it all taken care of.

So the weight got heavier and heavier. I was afraid to leave home, but equally afraid to tell my dad I wasn't leaving. And now it was September already—there was only so long I could believably say that school just hadn't started yet. Something had to happen.

Maybe I could go in January. Or next fall. Maybe if I had some more time to think about it, I could do it. See, this was the other reason I didn't want my dad to hire Quinn. I'd kinda been hoping we just wouldn't find anyone to take my place and then that would be my excuse to explain why I had to postpone school. Now what was I gonna do? I just knew this Quinn guy was gonna mess up my life.

23. Quinn

IN THE WEE WEE *hours, that's when I think of you...*

Chuck Berry's lazy blues wafted off my mom's beat-up turntable. All I had to play on it was her old vinyl records, but I'd come to like a lot of them, and I also liked how it made my room feel like a little time capsule, separate from the rest of the world.

The rest of the house been asleep for hours, but I was still sitting at my messy drafting table in a cloud of smoke. A manila envelope, stuffed with the drawings for my almost-completed book, leaned against one leg of the desk, addressed to Steve's Komix. A scrawled post-it stuck to it said, "Cait, when you find this, please mail ASAP."

Desperate to finish my book, but still unable to draw, I sat there madly ripping and pasting pieces of miscellaneous past drawings—unused sketches, partial studies—into collaged sheets, combining them with pictures ripped from magazines in a panicked pursuit of additional images. It felt like if I worked fast enough, hard enough, maybe I could fend off the fever dreams—which is what I was convinced they were—waking dreams caused by something backing up inside my head. By images that couldn't find their way out my fingers onto a page. Either that, or I was losing my mind.

The panel I was obsessing over showed the Black Dog running through deep blue shadows in a maze of alleys and abandoned buildings. The Demon Boy was nowhere in sight.

As I worked, I became increasingly aware of the sound of rain outside. It grew louder and louder, until it was inescapable, permeating the room. Every muscle in my body grew tense, bracing for what I feared was coming.

In a wee little room, I sit alone and think of you...

And the drawing detonated off the page, filling the room around me with swirling, three-dimensional action. Demon Boy tore through the room setting small fires in his wake. The dog chased him, its ragged breathing cutting through the sound of the rain like a serrated knife. It felt frantic, disorienting. Half-standing, I staggered back against my chair, trying to get out of their way.

Shadow Man burst in, tall and imposing, the perfect vigilante anti-hero. He surveyed the room, and his eyes narrowed as he spotted the Demon Boy, his prey. A voice emanated from him— he wasn't exactly speaking because he had no mouth—but words seeped from him like a cold fog that I felt in my bones.

This will be our final confrontation.

Demon Boy dashed past me, laughing, his red eyes glowing. Shadow Man sent the dog racing after him. The dog cornered Demon Boy, who looked a little bit afraid for the first time. Shadow Man slowly approached, unsheathing a sword made of utter darkness.

"*Are you ready?*" he asked, his blade of oblivion poised above the Demon Boy's head. The Demon Boy suddenly opened his mouth wide, forming a perfect circle, and let loose a hideous, fiery scream...

I threw down the drawings I'd been clutching in my puffy, bruised hand, unable to drop them fast enough. I was shiny with sweat. I looked around the room at nothing; they were gone. Chuck Berry was still singing.

One little song, for a fading memory...

I crossed the room and turned the music off. Now it was just me and the rain. I flipped a cigarette into my mouth, lit it with trembling hands, and sunk back into my desk chair.

24. Quinn

So far, it had only happened at night, and by the next morning, I was feeling better. Just thinking about my plan to off myself put me in an unexpectedly good mood—though I'd promised myself I had to stick around long enough to finish my damn book. Then, remembering that, in the meantime, I'd taken a job that was the exact opposite of something Caitlin would call "safe" made me feel downright giddy.

Some corny seventies song was playing on a tinny old radio in the back workroom at the butcher shop. The radio was bound in place in the corner of the windowsill by spider webs so old that the original spider probably listened to this song the first time around, and the round knobs were covered with dried bloody fingerprints. Mr. Raffallo had given me some big slabs of meat to trim, and I was having a good time, bopping around to the music and hacking off hunks of meat. I'd had to leave my air cast at home, of course, and my bad wrist was wobbly, but I worked around it as best as I could.

From the back room, I had a good view out to the front counter where two old ladies were waiting to be served by Mr. Raffallo and Reese. I recognized them from around the neighborhood, and they saw me looking at them and whispered to each other. I knew what they were probably saying, but was in such an unusually good mood that I just smiled and waved a bloody hand at them. One waved back, uncomfortably.

The song ended and an irritating commercial came on, so I rolled the knob and changed the station. I found a twangy country song—old school, not this Top 40 country-pop bullshit that's popular now—and turned it up. I was dancing around, singing along, and chopping into my side of beef when Mr. R loomed in the doorway.

"Hey! It's 'EASY 106' or you turn it off," he roared.

"Sorry, Daddy!" Reese rushed in past her father, and switched the station back. Mr. R returned to the ladies at the front counter, slightly embarrassed in the wake of his outburst.

"He doesn't like country music," Reese said to me quietly.

"Loud and clear," I said, with a little salute.

Reese was rocking a totally new look—she was wearing her butcher's apron over a pink wool Jacqueline Kennedy suit, complete with pillbox hat. I thought, *This girl must be nuts with all these outfits.* Then I thought, *I wonder which personality you would end up with if you managed to get her outfit off?* Should I not tell you that? I'm never sure which comments are the ones that make people hate me, but I think that might be one. I'm just being honest, and honest either gets me into trouble or into bed—though I can never really predict which. Like I said, I'm not that good at reading people.

"I like the outfit *du jour*," I said, getting back to cubing the meat.

Still standing in the doorway, she adjusted the buttons on her suit, the tilt of her hat. "It's Jackie O."

"Yeah, I got that." I smiled a little, gesturing to her bloody apron, "With a little bit of JFK."

She looked down at herself. "Oh no… I didn't even… You think it's in bad taste? Maybe I should change."

"Nah, statute of limitations on taste has run out."

I saw her staring at my hands. They were moving quickly, the knife blade whizzing so fast you could hardly track it. I wasn't super-accurate, but I was confident.

"I've been working here half my life and I can't do that," she said.

I kept slicing. "If I put a two-by-four piece of wood on the ground, could you walk across it without falling off?" I asked.

"Uh…yeah."

"Could you do it fifty feet in the air?"

"I don't think I'd want to find out," she said, not following my argument.

"It's the same walk—what's the difference?"

"Well, the *height*, for one…"

"Nope. The attitude. No fear, no danger."

"So you can chop that meat because you've got attitude?"

I shrugged. "I don't know. You're impressed, though, right?"

"Mildly entertained."

Mr. R's voice boomed from the front counter, "Theresa! I need Mrs. Varon's order from the freezer!"

I followed her into the walk-in freezer. "Do you need help?"

"No, I got it."

I went in anyway. I'm not totally sure why. I like a challenge, I guess.

✖

THE WALK-IN WAS LIKE a little cave of meat. Metal shelves were piled high with brown paper–wrapped packages. Large cuts, ribboned with fat and muscle, hung from the ceiling, so heavy they barely budged when you shouldered your way past them. Tall rolling racks held stacks of metal trays, packed with smaller cuts.

While Reese was looking through a pile of labeled orders, I pulled a large, naked leg of lamb off one of the trays and held it up.

"Don't you ever wonder what humans taste like?"

She looked at me sideways. "Is that your idea of flirting?"

"I just mean, chop us up and freeze us and this is all we are, right here." I waggled the frozen sheep leg back and forth, like it was walking around. That really made her mad for some reason.

"No we're *not*."

"What's the difference, throw some skin on top and there you go."

"I can't explain it, we're just different." Frowning, she spun and walked out of the freezer.

"Hey, I was just messing around…"

She turned around again, her back against the open door, and looked at me for a long time, like she was searching for clues. "You're weird," she finally said.

"You're one to talk. Do you want to go out sometime?" I wasn't planning to say that, it just sort of popped out of my mouth.

See, I had had no intention of messing with her, or any other girls at this point. I needed to focus on finishing my book so I could go through with my plan. The butcher shop job was to buy some time and entertain myself in the meantime, but I had decided I definitely didn't have time for girls. But this one… She was different, but I wasn't sure why. I didn't know what she was—she threw me off balance.

"Do I want to go out? *Why?*" she asked.

See what I mean? That just stumped me. "Uh…for fun…?"

"No, thanks." She turned to leave the freezer.

Her dad yelled, "Theresa! Where are you, I need that order!"

"Coming, Daddy!"

I remembered something that seemed, at that moment anyway, to explain everything. And I felt, if I didn't say it, the conversation between us would be over forever. I didn't know how to say it, but she'd already stepped out and the freezer door was closing, so I just winged it.

"At the bar. When I put the cigarette out. You were...neutral. Most people, they're either repelled or attracted. I just... I guess I want one or the other from you."

She caught the freezer door with her hand, stopping it from shutting, and poked her head back in.

"You don't prefer one or the other?"

"No." I really didn't, usually. But this time, I nervously realized, I might.

Her meathead brother, who I'd finally learned had a name—Donny—came back and grabbed the customer's order from her arms.

"We need you up front, not having a tea party back here." He gave me a knife-sharp glare and returned to the front with the package.

"Clearly, he's not my biggest fan," I joked to Reese, not sure where we had left things. Now I just wished I hadn't said anything at all.

"Donny is...kind of an idiot savant. Except without the savant part. Listen, I'm going to this street fair thing tonight. The Festival of Saint Rocco. I'm going and you're welcome to come along."

She turned abruptly and left the freezer. The door shut with a loud *thunk*. I wasn't positive what had just happened, but I seemed to have a date. So I figured I'd postpone swearing off girls until right after this one. It wouldn't last long—because once they got to know me better, it never did—and the rest of my plan could stay reassuringly in place.

25. Caitlin

SOME POOR GUY'S CHEST was spread wide open, his insides on the outside, wet and red and pulsing. Clamps and sponges and metal instruments, each with a single job to do, were silently passed across his unconscious body as classical music played.

"*Wham! Wham! Wham!*—he bangs three aces in a row, and I started to lose it. My backhand fell to shit…"

"You can't let that stuff get to you. The moment your emotions take over, you're dead."

The interns and nurses feigned interest in the doctors' conversation, but Caitlin, standing just behind the lead surgeon's right shoulder, passing him tools from a draped metal tray, was too tired to even pretend. She glanced over at the patient's vitals monitor. *Bounce… Bounce…*

"Caitlin?"

"Sorry?"

"Heart rate?" he snapped.

"Seventy-six and steady."

The monitor bounced happily on.

✶

She helped four-year-old Quinn, in his rubber-soled Superman pajamas, drag pieces of plywood into place, building a small ramp over an oblivious, panting golden retriever. Blondie. That placed her memory firmly in time because they had only had Blondie for a short while when she was eleven. A therapist had suggested a dog as a way for Quinn to learn physical empathy for others, a way to understand how delicate animals and people both are, but their mom had given Blondie away after only a couple of months. She had said it was because they didn't have time to care for her properly, but Caitlin was pretty sure it was because the dog had chewed her mother's good shoes. Even though Blondie was "Quinn's dog," Caitlin had whispered all of her secrets into Blondie's velvety ears, and was silently gutted when she disappeared.

That morning in their side driveway, she helped Quinn build the ramp so she could shoot his jump with her dad's video camera, the new one he had gotten himself for Christmas. At eleven, she had briefly thought she might want to make movies someday, a fantasy that she never dared share with anyone, and which soon faded. But when she remembered that day, it was through that lens; the memory looked like a home video.

Quinn grinned into the camera for a moment, then sprinted off and jumped onto a plastic Big Wheel. Caitlin swung the camera around, catching a glimpse of their frantic mother hurrying toward the scene, then quickly whipped it back to Quinn, to capture him already racing toward the ramp.

Blondie, alarmed, scooted out of the way just before Quinn sailed up the ramp; he seemed to hover for a long joyful moment...and then crashed face-first onto the driveway. Their mother paused, mid-step, momentarily frozen with panic, as their father came storming out of the house and past her, furious. Quinn pushed himself up off the concrete, blood pouring from his mouth, his front two teeth broken—and smiled. With one hand, their father hauled Quinn roughly off the ground, and with the other snatched the camera away from Caitlin and delivered an angry slap.

Caitlin remembered that the last thing she had been recording on the camera before it was switched off by her father was a sideways shot of Quinn, covered in his own blood, holding his arms up in a V-for-victory pose, and beaming before an imagined ovation. She knew it was wrong somehow, but she loved that image, that instant in time. She couldn't think of a moment she could remember Quinn looking happier.

She thought she would be in trouble mainly for taking her dad's camera without permission, but when she was locked in her room without dinner to "think about what she did," it was made abundantly clear that her crime was that she hadn't prevented Quinn from hurting himself. That was when it crystalized, when it became evident to her that she was expected to be responsible for him.

Within a year, both Blondie and their mom would be gone, and Caitlin obediently filled both vacant spots.

✖

A WAVE OF HEAT hit her and she felt like she suddenly had no bones. Her body went all floppy and she felt fairly positive she was about to faint or throw up. "Excuse me, I'm not feeling well. Candy, can you cover for a minute…?" She knew this was nearly inexcusable to do in the middle of surgery, and avoided their scowls as she hurried out of the operating room before something worse could happen.

She ran through two doors, out of the surgical suite, and into the recovery wing, stripping off her gown and mask. She stood in the outer hallway, gasping for air like she had been underwater. She drank from the water fountain, took a deep breath, and tried to refocus. She saw a nurse at the station down the hall counting out pills into little paper cups on a rolling cart, preparing to distribute them to patients in the wing. Another nurse called out a question from down the hall and the meds nurse walked away to talk to her, leaving the cart just sitting there. Alone and unattended. It may as well have had a giant spotlight on it. Caitlin couldn't look away. She walked coolly down the hall toward it, calculating how many Vicodins she could palm without it being noticeable. Six feet away. Three feet away. Her hand reaching out. Just as she curled her fingers around a few pills, the meds nurse reappeared.

"They done with that valve replacement already?" she asked Caitlin. "I don't have a bed ready yet."

"You've got a good half hour, "Caitlin replied as casually as she could manage, as she pulled her hand back and dropped the three pinched pills into her pocket. Had the nurse seen anything? Was that suspicion in her gaze, or just innocent curiosity?

"Alright then." The meds nurse went back to counting out pills. Caitlin feigned fascination with the patient information white board on the wall for a moment, then reversed direction and headed back toward the operating room.

Wham! Wham! Wham! Three little pills. She'd take one now, have two left for emergencies—*or for tomorrow, whichever came first,* she joked to herself, feeling giddy. The only other time she had stolen something was when she took a lip gloss at the mall when she was thirteen—and, overcome with guilt, had returned to the store and reverse shoplifted it back onto the shelf the next day. She wouldn't return the pills, obviously, but she promised herself she definitely wouldn't do that again. It was a one-time, opportunistic, impulsive thing just to get her through a temporary, difficult time. As she walked, she popped one Vicodin in her mouth and swallowed it dry, while fingering the remaining two reassuringly inside her pocket.

She entered her code into the keypad to get back into the surgical suite, pulled a fresh sterile pack off the shelf and started scrubbing back in.

26. Quinn

FOR FOUR BLOCKS, THE street was closed off to cars, and a banner declared it the "Festival of St. Rocco." It seemed like every month was a different festival for some Italian saint or another—this guy sounded like the patron saint of broken noses, if you asked me. Overhead, crisscrossed strings of globe lights blazed; below them, the street swirled with the electricity of a crowd looking for a good time.

Me and Reese weaved our way through the swarm of people, past the creaky tilt-a-whirl, the seductive smells of competing food vendors, and the kids twirling neon lassos. She was wearing a suede fringe number, sort of a Patsy Cline look. I thought things were looking pretty promising. She was going on and on about this Saint Rocco.

"So after Rocco's parents died, he decided to devote his life to caring for victims of the plague. This was back, you know, when the plague was like a common part of everyday life."

I nodded my head like I was really into it.

"Then Rocco got the plague himself, but, miraculously, he recovered…and then he went on to heal a whole bunch of other people."

"Well, ninety percent of all medical problems will just go away on their own if they're left untreated," I pointed out. I mean, sorry, it was true. "The other ten percent will kill you, of course—"

She frowned at me. "They had the *plague*. So when Rocco finally returned to his own village, he had been gone so long that his uncle didn't recognize him and threw Rocco in jail, thinking he was a spy. And he was in jail for five years."

"Why didn't he just say who he was? 'Dude, it's me, Rocco!' Come on, *Rocco!*"

"Do you want to hear this or not?"

"Yes, it's very impressive."

"So Rocco died in jail, and only after he'd died did the uncle find out it was him because he recognized the birthmark in the shape of the cross on Rocco's chest."

"So he's a saint because he had a birthmark?"

"No, because he healed people. Forget it, I just thought it was cool."

"Yeah, it's cool. I never realized how cool obscure dead saints could be. Hey, you wanna see something *really* cool?" I flipped my lit cig up into my mouth with my tongue and back out again, letting out a puff of smoke as a *ta-da* flourish. A party trick, but people always freaked out for it.

She just looked at me and said, "Don't do that. Please."

"It's just a trick," I mumbled.

Something caught her eye in a doorway behind the security grate of a closed storefront. She squeezed through the barrier between a busy calzone booth and an even busier short-handed kettle corn stand, and knelt down next to the grate. I followed her.

"Oh my God, look how skinny." It was a scrawny, three-legged cat with a couple of mangy bald spots. She offered it a scrap of soft pretzel off the ground but it hissed at her.

"Leave it alone," I said.

"He's starving. Your arms are longer, see if you can grab him."

I didn't really want to touch this cat—and it didn't want me touching it either. When I put my arm through the grate, it growled and attacked me. I swatted back at it.

"Damn strays—they should all just be put to sleep," I grumbled, standing up again.

She stared at me, dumbfounded. "How can you say that?"

"It's never gonna be a normal, rub-up-against-you, give-me-my-Friskies kittycat."

"Maybe not, but with a good home and some love…"

"It's too late—he's not socialized. You can't rehabilitate strays—try to do something nice for them and they freakin' bite you." I could feel myself slipping into a rant, and I knew in the back corner of my mind that this was not going to be good for my chances with this girl, but I couldn't stop myself. For some reason this stupid cat had tapped into something that made me feel hot and uncomfortable in my chest. "He's an outcast, a survival machine. What's the point of being alive if all you do is limp around trying to give people rabies?"

"Well, why is *anyone* alive?"

"Exactly. Either have a good reason, or stop taking up space."

"Well, maybe there's a higher purpose we don't know about yet. How would you like it if someone decided *you* were useless and didn't deserve to live?"

"I'd load the gun for them."

Ahh, crap. Too far. She was on the verge of tears.

"Go on ahead. Go," she said quietly. "I'm gonna try to catch him."

I just stood there and watched as she reached for the cat, murmuring, "Hey, hey, hey, it's okay, shhhh…" It took a swipe at her, raking red scratches across her hand, then squeezed through a gap in the grate and disappeared into the darkness.

She looked up at me and I shrugged, thinking I really should try to keep my thoughts to myself for the rest of the night. She stood up and we walked back into the spin and eddy of the festival without saying anything at all.

✖

WE PASSED SOME STREET performers, the kind you see in all the touristy areas, Faneuil Hall, Harvard Square, whatever: hiphop acrobats cartwheeling over each other while rap blared from portable speakers, a dude in a kilt, riding a unicycle while playing bagpipes. We didn't have anything to say to each other so it was a relief to just stop and watch something, anything. We gravitated over to a large crowd that was watching a young fire-eater. Heavy metal blared from a boom box as he did what seemed to be his big finale: allowing audience members to toast marshmallows off the five-foot plume of flame shooting from his mouth. Big applause for that one. He took a bow and spat out the residue of whatever nasty fuel was in his mouth, then worked the front edge of the crowd, high-fiving and passing a hat.

"Please feel free to express your appreciation monetarily, folks. And stick around for the always-popular Human Pincushion!"

Somewhere behind me, I dimly heard Reese say, "No thanks, I'll pass," but I was already pushing through the crowd to get up to the front. This I wanted to see.

✖

HE LOOKED LIKE AN Iggy Pop who had never discovered punk rock. Whatever manic spark he might've once had seemed to have been repeatedly dampened until it was barely an ember. His body was lean, pale, and tired. A dozen small needles, each about two inches long with a tiny primary-colored sphere on one tip, were already laced through the skin on his face, in a line down his forehead, and fanning out across both cheeks.

Now he stood on an upside-down plastic milk crate, dressed only in a pair of too-small gym shorts, waving two foot-long needles in exaggerated gestures and muttering elaborate but uninspired patter as he prepared to slide them in and through his slack belly skin.

Then he stopped talking and in they went, easily and silently. The tips of the needles reemerged a few inches from their entry point.

"Ew," said someone in the crowd. Several people walked away.

Then, still impaled, he reached over and rummaged around in a big faded duffel bag. He stood up brandishing a long, thin and glinty sword and announced that he was going to attempt to push it in through one of his cheeks and back out the other.

"Do it, do it, do it!" chanted a herd of middle school boys.

He claimed he was not sure he could, and pretended to struggle to get it through, but I could see the scars on his cheeks, and it was clear that he had done this so many times before that he had no choice but to be either dead bored or drunk or both, just to get through the performance.

Reese whispered to me, "That is so totally fake," but I shook my head no. I couldn't take my eyes off him.

✖

WHEN THE ACT ENDED and the crowd started to disperse in search of the next distraction, Reese said something about wanting to find a bathroom. I said yeah yeah I'd meet her back here and walked over to the edge of the fair. I stood between two parked cars and gazed into a desolate parking lot lit by sickly yellow streetlights where I thought I had seen him go.

"'Scuze me, buddy." Someone shoved my shoulder and I hopped aside to let them pass, and it was him. The Pincushion Man. He'd thrown on a ratty old robe and was clutching his duffel bag and a handful of his long needles. I followed, trailing about twenty feet behind him, till he reached an old brown van that, from the looks of it, was also his home. As he slid the heavy door open, I saw inside: patchy shag carpeting, fast food wrappers, a saggy air mattress, a bong, and a bony old dog. He climbed in and started to slide the door shut, so I made my move.

"Sir? Excuse me, sir?"

The Pincushion Man turned around, unfiltered cigarette dangling from his lip. I walked close enough to distinguish the different notes of pot smoke, wet dog, and stale beer wafting from the van.

"Yeah?" he crabbed.

"I saw your show."

He just blinked at me.

"It was great."

"I can't tell you how much that means to me," he slurred sarcastically. The bony dog barked once. The sliding door slammed shut.

I sat down on the curb. I felt like I needed to say or do something more. I wasn't really sure why, but I needed to talk to him. Between my feet, half-laying in a murky, oily puddle, was a old, forgotten, foot-long needle. I picked it up and rolled it between my fingers.

✖

I WAS STANDING THERE for about five minutes before I saw movement behind the little curtain in the van's window, a hand pulling the nubby orange fabric aside and a watery eye peering out at me. He dropped the curtain and pulled the sliding door open with a screech, a half-empty can of beer in his hand.

"What the Jesus are you doing?" he shouted at me.

I was standing next to the van, holding up my forearm and pulling the rusty needle slowly back and forth through it like a violin bow. I pulled the needle all the way out—it came free with a tiny pop—and held it up to him.

"When you do this, does it hurt?" I asked.

"Where'd you get that? Give it to me." He reached out to grab the needle, but I held it behind my back.

"Does it *hurt?*" I asked again.

He seemed to comprehend, even through his beer haze, how urgently I needed an answer.

"No," he said.

I didn't move, unsure what to say or do now. I hadn't thought beyond my question, though a million things were ping-ponging off the walls of my skull. The Pincushion Man turned to go back inside his van.

"I'm the same way. I'm like you," I blurted.

He stopped short, turned around and studied my face. He took his cigarette out of his mouth and pensively picked a piece of tobacco off his tongue. The alcohol stink coming off him was staggering.

"Oh, you got the talent alright, I see that," he said, "but we don't need no two Pincushion acts."

"No, you don't understand..."

"Oh, I understand, 'cause it couldn't be more obvious— you see this and you think: the glamour, the excitement, the pussy—oh yeah, don't tell me you don't know the chicks dig this shit. But if you chose this life, then you sure as hell better move somewhere else. Me and Doug—the fire guy—we started doing the freak show thing at those Lollapalooza dealies—and now we travel the street circuit up here: Boston, New York, Philly. You gotta take your act somewhere else—California or something. Venice Beach, you know? Weather's nice, bikinis, rollerblades, all that David Lee Roth shit. Go, you'll love it."

He paused to drain the last of his beer. I wasn't sure if he was done, but I piped up, thinking I could redirect his misconception, "No, I just—"

"You even know who he is, David Lee Roth?" Christ, he wasn't done. "What a moron that guy is. Should have kept his mouth shut and cut his hair way earlier, like Bon Jovi, the times they were a-changin', but no… Lurked around for twenty years waiting for a Van Halen reunion—move on, dude, move on! But, you know, you make choices in life, you gotta live with 'em. Like, I been doing this so long, I couldn't do nothing else—you know how they say when you're small, you make a face you'll stick like that, and that's fine—but just know what you're getting into, is all. And cut your damn hair when you start looking like an old afghan hound."

"No, you don't understand, I'm not trying to take your job—I just thought…maybe you were like me."

He sneered. "If you want a freakin' soulmate, you're knockin' on the wrong door."

The bony dog barked again. The Pincushion Man plucked his rusty needle from my hand and disappeared back into his van, slamming the door in my face.

"Wait! When did…"

"Why are you bothering that poor man?"

I whirled around. It was Reese. She looked confused—and annoyed.

"I'm not. I just, uh, wanted to see how he did it," I sputtered.

"It was pretty creepy, that's all I need to know."

I didn't say anything. She wouldn't understand. I didn't even really understand. We walked wordlessly back toward the festival. When I glanced back at the van, though, I swear I saw the Pincushion Man watching me from behind the little curtain.

27. Quinn

S WE WANDERED BACK into the main stream of fair-goers, Reese said she wanted some fried dough, so she went ahead and got in line. I wanted to think about what just happened a little more, so I told her I was gonna have a cig and wait for her off to the side. As I was lighting up, I spotted Reese's brother Donny sitting over on the post office steps with two neighborhood guys I'd seen around, Mikey and Brandon, swigging beers out of paper bags and watching the St. Rocco's crowd filter past.

Donny leaned out and called out to a hot girl walking by, arm-in-arm with two slightly less hot girlfriends. "Hey, sweetheart, you like fresh Italian sausage?" Mikey and Brandon snickered and hooted.

"Oh, is that what that is?" the hot girl shouted back at him, "I was lookin' for a toothpick 'cause I thought it was a cocktail weenie!" She and her two friends shot the guys flying double-handed middle fingers as they walked away.

The guys were stunned for a moment, then erupted into loud, demented laughter.

"Six fingers! A record!" crowed Brandon, compulsively pinching up the spikes in his hair to make sure they were perfect, a tic that seemed to intensify when he got all keyed up.

"You crack me up to no frickin' end, man, you really do," muttered Mikey, shaking his head at Donny's sheer awesomeness.

Reese wandered toward me, eating her fried dough, and I immediately steered her in the opposite direction from these mouth breathers—she didn't see them, but goddamnit, they spotted her.

"Isn't that your sister over there? Hey now…" leered Brandon.

I listened with one ear as we fought the upstream crowd, not making much forward progress.

"Quit it, no one's messing with my sister," decreed Donny.

"Well that's not what I'm spying with my little eye over here." I looked back to see Brandon pointing at us with his eyebrows and Donny looking over; he caught my eye for a split second before I glanced away

Mikey piped up, excited to tell Donny something he might not know. "You know this guy?"

"Why?" Donny said warily.

"He was a grade or two behind us at Central til he dropped out. Guy's a fuckin' freak show…"

"Like how?" demanded Brandon, feverishly spiking his hair up.

We got out of earshot, and I didn't hear the rest, but I didn't need to. I nudged Reese gently, trying to get her to walk a little faster.

A moment later, I saw Donny in my peripheral vision, shouldering his way through the crowd to catch up with us. My skin prickled with adrenaline but I made myself take a breath. Maybe if we just said hello and kept moving…

"You hitting on my sister?" huffed Donny.

Reese was mortified. "Donny, he's not… This isn't…"

"I'm not talking to you." He got right in my face. "Are you hitting on my sister?"

"No." My calmness pissed Donny off. Smug son of a bitch was asking for it.

"You better not be, you stupid freak."

The last word rippled through my body like an electric shock. We faced off, staring at each other for a long moment; it felt like we were both acutely aware of where this was going, preparing for a dance we both knew. Donny moved first, aiming a low punch to my gut, but I saw it coming and darted out with my hand—the bad one—and deflected him. Donny grabbed my bad wrist and bent it back ninety degrees. I roundhoused with the other good fist and *POW!* A good one, landing solidly on the corner of Donny's square face. That was Brandon and Mikey's cue to jump into the mix, three on one.

"Stop it!" screamed Reese.

She kicked Mikey hard in the crotch, taking him out of commission.

I landed a solid headbutt to Brandon's forehead and Brandon crumpled to the ground, his gelled hair spikes still intact. I immediately turned back to Donny, who was coming back at me. We grappled and fell to the ground, scrambling for the upper hand. A crowd formed around us, taking cell phone pictures and yelling.

"Stop it, both of you!" shouted Reese. I saw her grab onto the sleeve of Donny's jacket but he shrugged her off.

Donny got a good hold on me and slammed my head on the pavement; I saw double for a second, but managed to roll Donny over and deliver a nice vicious punch to his eye.

"ENOUGH OF THIS BULLSHIT! KNOCK IT OFF!" A giant bald mountain of a security guard stepped into the gladiator circle and pulled me off Donny. I reluctantly let go of Donny's shirt, and Donny slumped back on the ground, conscious but thrashed.

28. Quinn

EESE AND I SAT next to each other on a low brick wall, both a little stunned in the aftermath of the fight. She wiped some blood from my cheek with a crumpled paper napkin and her hand was tiny and delicate and unexpectedly soft. I figured she had been on my side; after all, *he* had confronted *me*. I thought that maybe the fight could work out in my favor and that the evening could be turning around.

"I'm sorry, Donny is kind of overprotective sometimes. I think he was dipped a little too long in the macho vat."

"It's alright."

"Are you sure you feel okay?"

"Yeah, positive."

"You were so...*good* at that." I couldn't tell if she meant it as just a straightforward statement of fact, or as a compliment. So I took it as the latter. It seemed like she wasn't an exception after all—she was one of these girls who liked tough-guy shit. Especially when it was over her. This I knew how to deal with. This was a car I knew how to drive.

"Oh, yeah?" I asked.

"Yeah."

When I glanced over at her, I saw her for a quick second as I would have drawn her if she'd been a superhero—ultra-sexy and busting out of her fringed jacket. And her avatar winked at me. So I kissed her—for real.

I realized when she pulled away, startled, that maybe I had misread her. There was a way, way awkward silence.

I needed to say something.

Anything.

"So…how do you know all that about Saint Rocky, or whatever?"

She looked at her lap. "Church. And it's Rocco, actually. Rocco."

More silence.

"Well, maybe you can take a class on all that stuff in college."

"Yeah," she said flatly.

"Don't sound *too* excited about it."

"I'm not. I mean, I am, but I'm not, if you know what I mean."

I didn't, so I just nodded.

"I don't know, I might, like, put it off or something. Maybe go next year instead. Don't take it personally, but I was hoping my dad wouldn't find anyone to take my place in the shop."

"Why?"

"He needs me. I take care of him, I do all the bookkeeping… It's complicated."

"Can't Donny do that?"

"Maybe… But it's not that. I just feel bad about leaving him. He's my dad. Know what I mean?"

I didn't, really. "Yeah, sure. My dad…he actually died last week." I was going for shock value, but I immediately realized I'd opened a conversational door I really didn't want to go through. I lit a cig and nervously played with the still-lit match as we talked. Deflect, distract, discourage.

"Oh my god, I'm sorry. Were you close to him?"

"No."

"Oh. What about your mom?"

"She left when I was five. Why are you so nosy?" That last part came out sounding more aggressive than it had been in my mind a split second before, and I saw her draw back a little. I wasn't trying to lose her entirely, just to change the subject.

I saw her glance over at the match I was still fiddling with; I hadn't noticed that the tiny flame was so close to my fingertips that it had made a charred patch on my thumb. I saw her seeing it and quickly pinched out the little burning nub. Deflect, deflect.

"Do you have a lot of stuffed animals on your bed at home?"

"What kind of question is that?" she said, on the defensive. "No. Some. Not a lot."

"Aren't you afraid Mr. and Mrs. Teddy Bear will miss you if you go away to school?"

"What are you talking about?"

"Seems like as good a made-up reason as any for you not to go."

She just stared at me. Yeah, I'd hit a sore spot. Bull's-eye.

"I'm not making up a reason. I just care about my dad. Apparently, this is a strange concept to you."

"Caring about people just backfires on you. It's a trap, a crutch, a weakness."

"What an asshole-y thing to say."

"Are you calling me an asshole?"

"Kind of, yeah."

I thought that over. I was just telling the truth, not specifically trying to be a dick. "Insensitive, probably, people have definitely called me that before, but I don't know if I'd go as far as 'asshole.'"

"It's the same thing."

A sharp goaty laugh leapt out of the darkness. I looked up and saw that hipster girl Sydney walking by, arm-in-arm with some ridiculous dude with skinny jeans and questionable facial hair.

"Well, look who's here," Sydney cackled. As she walked past, she squinted a little at Reese, recognizing her. "Wow, wouldn't have predicted that. She didn't seem like your type."

Oh great.

"Just ignore her," I muttered to Reese.

"Wait, I wanna know, what type is that?" Reese called after her.

"Oh, you know, kinda…twisted," Sydney replied. She turned around in the street and put on an insincerely sweet tone that made me want to throw something at her. "Just, you know, between girls—I'd watch out for him."

As they walked away, the guy she was with scowled, "You know that weirdo?"

Reese turned to me. "That's that girl from the bar. What was *that* all about?"

"Nothing, she's kind of a psycho or something."

"Did you do something with her?"

I mumbled something that didn't contain any actual words.

She looked around, like she was hoping for an exit door from reality. "You know, I really should go."

She jumped down off the wall and started walking away. Deflection had maybe gone too far. Ugh, this kind of thing was so much harder to navigate when you cared even a tiny bit about the outcome. I knew it was a long shot, but thought it might still be possible to salvage something.

"Look, I'm not that good at this. I'm not that good at anything. Except maybe drawing. I know you think I'm kind of a jerk, but, do you wanna, like…come over or something?"

She turned around and stared at me like I was an alien. Or an idiot. Or an idiot alien.

"Come over? Does anything in this picture make you think this is going at all well?"

I had another quick flash of the cartoon version of her, but this time her ultra-sexy avatar hauled back and punched me in the nose.

The real Reese was satisfied just pummeling me with words though. "You know, when the evening started out, I had some hope. But it's gone seriously downhill. I mean..." She ticked them off on her hand, "...you're running off talking to circus freaks, lecturing me about killing all the stray cats, you barely ask me anything about myself, but somehow still manage to insult my whole...life, and random passing girls stop and warn me about you like I'm in some spy movie—and now you expect me to come back and like sleep with you or something? I don't know what world you're living in, but back here in real life, there are other people who have their own ideas and feelings, and it might be good if you noticed that every now and then."

She turned to go, but then realized she had more to say. "I don't know why, but I thought you might be weird-good, but you're not. You're weird-bad. Weird–messed up. Weird-mean."

I thought back to the moment when she was looking at me with that oddly neutral expression in the bar. "So...the whole attracted/repelled thing—it seems you've come down solidly in the repelled camp?" I smiled, making a joke of it.

She walked away.

I was left alone with my cig and that same weird flip-flopping feeling in my stomach that I remembered having the day before, when I was showing Steve my drawings.

With Steve, I guess it was because I wanted him to like my work. I'll cop to that. But mostly I didn't care what people thought of me—especially in situations with girls. So why was I so irked by what had just happened? Girls had rejected me before, all the time. But this seemed different somehow. Maybe because what she said wasn't about whether she thought I was cute or cool or whatever—who cares, no accounting for taste, etcetera etcetera—but on account of who she thought I *was*. I had failed a test I didn't even know I was taking, which didn't seem fair at all. Self-centered? Isn't everyone?

I watched a couple walking by, holding hands, all cuddly and flirty. Not in that wound-up we-haven't-done-it-yet-but-are-so-gonna-real-soon way—more in a dreamy, we've-been-doing-it-for-a-while-and-are-deep-in-hormonally-induced-luuuurve kind of way. I had always blown that off as some kind of mutual brainwashing that couples talked themselves into, but now I just felt kind of puzzled. If you weren't self-centered, and you weren't brainwashed, and you really did willingly put your head in someone else's guillotine, weren't you cracked in a different way?

Achh, my stomach felt weird. I lit a new cig off the butt of the old one, hopped off the wall, and decided to take the long way home.

29. Reese

CREPT UP THE STAIRS to our apartment, trying to avoid the creaky floorboards, hoping to just get to bed without running into Donny.

I was surprised and kind of embarrassed that I had actually said some of those things out loud to Quinn, but mostly I was mad at myself for even thinking he might be the right kind of weird. When guys are hard to read, or strange, I always assume there is some deep inner explanation, some multidimensional universe that would rainbow out of them if I could just crack them open. Though it's not like I'd had a lot of experience with this. I'd never even had a real boyfriend, unless you count two weeks with Ricky Alvarez in the eighth grade. He'd asked if I wanted to "go out" and I said okay just because he always disappeared right after school and no one knew where he went, which gave him some mystery. There were rumors. One kid in my homeroom told me Ricky supposedly had built a secret clubhouse under a bridge that was stocked with video games and every Pop-Tart flavor there is, and mean Rena Rinkman told me she'd heard that he had a super-rare kind of leukemia and had to go and get all his blood removed and "cleaned" by machines at the hospital every day. Turned out the dumb truth was that he had to walk over to his mom's office and do homework in the reception area every day until it was time to go home. We kissed once, badly, before I decided he was almost as interesting as cardboard. After that, I concentrated on schoolwork and vowed to admire mystery boys from afar.

I waggled the key in the lock as quietly as I could, and the door swung open into our dark kitchen. The only light and sound in the apartment was what was drifting faintly down the hall from the TV in my dad's bedroom. So far so good. Donny was probably still out with his brainless friends.

I just wanted a little something sweet to eat before bed. I usually had a piece of chocolate stashed somewhere—one of my superhero skills was that I was able to only eat one little bite at a time without snarfing the whole thing, so I could generally make it last for a while—but I constantly was having to hide it in a new place so Donny didn't find it. I looked in some recent spots—at the back of the silverware drawer, behind the row of dried out condiment bottles on the door of the fridge. Nothing. I'd either forgotten where I last put it, or that moron had eaten it.

"I wanna talk to you."

"Holy crap, Donny—" I stood up so fast I scraped my forehead on the door of the little butter cubby. "Ow!" I rubbed my head.

Donny stood in the door to the hallway, blocking the route to my room. By the light of the refrigerator, I could see he was pretty beat up, and dead serious. I closed the fridge door, leaving us in darkness.

"It's really late, I need to go to sleep," I protested.

"I said I gotta talk to you."

"Well, I don't want to talk to you."

"Tough."

"Look, it's so not cool for you to go around wailing on people you don't like."

"You're heading off to college, you don't need to be hanging out with some freak."

"We aren't 'hanging out.' Believe me. And I don't even know what I'm doing with college anyway." Whoa, did I just say that? What was with my big mouth today?

"What do you mean you don't know?" he asked cautiously.

I knew this wasn't the best time or way to bring it up, but now it was too late. The metaphorical cat had slipped out the door.

"I just...don't know if I want to go yet." My trial balloon floated out of my mouth and up to the ceiling. There was a little pause while Donny registered it.

"What the hell are you talking about? Due to what? Is it because of this guy?"

"No! Forget I said anything about it, just leave me alone."

"You have to go, it'll kill Dad if you don't."

"I know, I'm gonna go, but just...maybe not yet. I don't know, don't say anything to Dad, okay? Right now, I really need to get some sleep." I tried to push casually past him, but he wouldn't budge.

"Reesie, come on. You have to go." He frowned and looked down at the floor, suddenly getting quiet and almost shy. He tapped his foot a couple of times on top of mine. "I'm not going to go to college. But you're the smart one."

"I know," I mumbled.

"But listen to me," he said, his jaw visibly tensing up again, "This guy is not for you."

"Trust me, I know that already." I squirreled around him and headed down the hall toward my room. He followed me.

"Reese, wait."

"I really don't need a lecture. Nothing's happening with him, and it's none of your business anyway."

"It *is* my business," he said, "*Listen.*"

I paused at the door to my room and gave him my best "this better be good" look.

And it was. Boy oh boy, it was.

30. Quinn

THAT NIGHT, I COULDN'T get to sleep. There was too much swirling around inside my head about what had just happened with Reese, and my encounter with the Pincushion Man. Normally, I was able to just shut out stuff I didn't want to think about, but it seemed like, lately, I couldn't do that so well. I was also afraid that the pictures would come alive again. It was happening more and more and it felt dangerous, unmanageable. I wasn't able to control what they did, like I could when they were just drawings. And I didn't want to think too much about what it might mean about my sanity.

It seemed to make sense to me that maybe if I could finish the ending of the stupid book, they would leave me alone—or at least then *I* could finally just disappear, so I wouldn't cause problems for anyone anymore. But I wanted to leave something behind, so I needed to focus. No more distractions from girls—just get through the days, buying time from Caitlin with my joke job, and finishing the damn book. Then I could check out.

I was lying in my bed, smoking. The only light on in the basement was the small metal reading lamp next to my bed, which was focused on my lap, where I was paging through the last drawings I had done before I'd hurt my drawing hand. I hadn't been able to get very far with my post-injury cut-and-paste collages because I really had no idea what came next. I was pretty sure the Shadow Man had to kill Demon Boy once and for all, defeating chaos and restoring order in the universe.

But I couldn't figure out how. It was the weirdest thing, almost like the little bastard wasn't letting me kill him. I stared and stared at the drawings, stuck.

I think I must have dozed off for a second, because my head jerked up when I thought I heard someone talking to me. I listened for a second, but it was silent, so I figured I had dreamt it. I smelled smoke and saw that my cig had burnt a little hole in my quilt when I'd nodded off. Shit. I stubbed the butt out and dunked the charred spot into a glass of water. I started gathering my drawings, which had slid off my lap, getting ready to put them away and get some sleep.

"Hey. Hey. Can you help me?" a small voice asked.

What the hell? I scanned the room and spotted a little shadowy shape crouched under my drawing table. Demon Boy. The tiny red points of his eyes burned through the darkness. I swung my legs out of bed and nervously crept over to my desk, peering underneath. Nothing there but the glowing red light of the power strip where my reading light was plugged in. I crawled under the desk and unplugged the power strip, pitching the room into blackness.

I crawled back into bed, and pulled the covers over my shoulder. At least I was finally sleepy. I closed my eyes, but then heard a weird rustling sound. And then the voice again.

"Please?" it said.

I opened my eyes and they were there. The red, glowing eyes. Demon Boy, under the drawing table again. We just stared at each other.

31. Quinn

IN THE MORNING, WHEN I figured everyone had left for work or school, I surfaced from the basement and shuffled around the kitchen, poured a big bowl of store-brand fake Frosted Flakes and put it on the table in the middle of the room while I got a mug and drained the lukewarm dregs of the coffee pot.

I heard heavy feet descending the front stairs and my face involuntarily squinched up into a scowl. Will and I had been avoiding each other as much as possible since our confrontation at the residential facility. He came into the kitchen, dressed for the firehouse. He did a little surprised pause when he saw me, but said nothing, just went around scooping up an annoyingly healthy breakfast to take to work—a banana and a Power Bar.

"How's the job?" he grunted at me.

"What do you care?" I asked.

Will puffed up his chest, almost taking the bait, then backed off. I turned and opened the refrigerator, got busy trying to excavate the milk.

"Later," Will muttered as he headed out the door.

I finally got the milk out of the fridge without anything falling out, turned around to pour it on my cereal, and stopped short. There, neatly placed across the rim of my cereal bowl, was a glossy, tri-fold brochure for the FamilyCare facility—happy idiots grinning on the front flap.

I stared at it for a long moment, then methodically tore that stupid brochure into confetti-sized pieces and sprinkled them into the bowl. I poured the milk over the cereal and confetti mixture, and stood over the table, calmly eating every sugary, papery bite.

32. Quinn

LOOKING OVER MY SHOULDER, and carrying a small metal container full of meat scraps, I made my way through the back room of the butcher shop and pushed my shoulder against the rear door. Something in the weather had changed overnight and as the heavy metal door swung open, a sharp gray chill rushed in and mugged me. Some feral cats skittered away down the alley. I dumped the meat onto the ground.

"Here you go."

The Black Dog was sitting there on the other side of the alley, watching me. Ignoring him wasn't making him go away, so I thought I'd try feeding him. He showed no interest in the meat. He just stared at me, panting. I didn't like it.

"What do you want from me?"

He didn't answer, so I went back inside. As the door shut with a thunk behind me, Donny stomped in; he was wearing dark glasses and carrying a roast under his arm like a football.

"I was just putting out some garbage," I said, trying not to sound defensive.

He tipped his glasses down so I could see his fierce black eye.

"You better watch your ass," he growled. He shoved the roast at me and marched back to the front counter. Somehow I just had to get through this day.

I brought the roast into the walk-in freezer. Reese was inside, holding her apron out like a basket and tossing in chicken parts. She was wearing a bright, flowery mini-dress with a little white cardigan sweater over it, a wide headband, and 1960s eye makeup that made her look like a cat. I had a lot of time to stand there checking out the outfit of the day because she was totally ignoring me. Finally, I just said something brilliant like "uh…hey."

She didn't even look up at me. She just said, "What's it like?"

"What?"

"You know."

"No. I don't."

I was really hoping she was talking about something else, but I was pretty sure she wasn't. A sense of dread trickled over me, like a thin, cold drizzle from a faucet above my head.

She turned toward me and pinched my arm hard. I was so surprised, I didn't think to fake flinch.

"What?" I said, trying for casual obliviousness.

"Donny told me." She walked out the freezer door with her apronful of chicken. I grabbed her by the arm and pulled her back in.

"Did he tell your dad?"

"No, I asked him to let me be the one to do that."

"Don't. He'll fire me."

"Exactly."

"Please?"

Her dad yelled, "Theresa! I need that chicken!"

She left without looking me in the eye.

33. Reese

I DUMPED THE CHICKEN INTO the front display case in front of my dad. He and Donny were waiting on half a dozen customers, weighing and slicing and hustling.

"Daddy, I need to talk to you," I said, quiet and serious.

When Quinn, who had followed me up to the front, heard this, he kicked the wall and retreated into the back room.

"Not now, Theresa, it is too busy," Daddy said. He turned to his impatient old lady customer, "You said breasts, right?"

"Yes, six, the freshest you have, and I'm wondering if you have some nice soppressata—is it possible to get a sample? I don't like when it's too peppery…"

"I have to talk to you now," I interrupted.

He turned to me, irritable, "Please be some help—go upstairs and finish the books so I can go to the bank at lunchtime."

"But—"

"Books now, talking later. "

"Maybe Donny should do the books for once," I protested. Daddy glanced over at Donny, who was losing a battle with a large piece of plastic wrap that kept sticking to itself—then looked back to me, like "see?"

"Fine," I said, resigned, turning to go.

"And tell Quinn not to leave his bag up front, I'm tripping on it." He kicked Quinn's knapsack and it slid across the floor toward me. Drawings spilled out the open zipper, fanning across the tile. I knelt to pick them up and felt the tornado of upset in my head spinning slower and slower as I looked at them. Even though the pages were all out of order, and some were only partly completed, they were just…stunning. Dramatic and emotional and gorgeous. I gathered them up, amazed. I knew this shouldn't change what I thought I needed to do, but it did change how I felt. I didn't want it to, but it did, in ten seconds flat. People were mysterious, and discovering something like the fact that they had ridiculous artistic talent felt like getting a step closer to unraveling the mystery. I wished I had mystery, strings another person could untangle, but was always afraid I didn't, which was probably another reason the drawings impressed me so much.

I hooked the knapsack over my shoulder and carried the pile of drawings into the back room, still leafing through them.

"Quinn?" I called out.

But he wasn't there. His apron lay in a heap on the ground and the back door to the alley was ajar.

✖

I pushed the door open and stepped out into the alley. The feral cats twirled affectionately around my legs.

"Hello babies, not right now."

I spotted Quinn halfway down the alley, walking away fast.

"Hey!" I shouted.

He didn't stop or look back.

"These drawings, are they yours?"

He paused and turned around.

"You left your knapsack. They fell out," I explained, suddenly feeling sort of embarrassed, like I had seen something too personal.

He strode back, took the bag and drawings from my hands, and walked away again.

"They're really beautiful. I had no idea," I said.

"Yeah, whatever." He kept walking.

I called after him again, "I didn't tell my dad."

He slowed to a stop, but didn't turn around, just looked down at his feet. "But Donny told you what I have?"

"Basically, I guess."

He nodded his head, thinking, his back still to me.

"But I'd like to hear it from you," I said softly.

He finally turned around and looked me in the eye. "You're not still mad?"

I squinched up my face, shifted my weight back and forth a couple of times before answering. "Well... I still think you were a total jerk last night."

"*But...*"

"But I want to understand it."

"Why, so you can explain it to your dad in medically correct terms?" he said, acidic and mean.

I just pulled at my headband, frustrated. "Can you drop the sarcastic thing for just a second?"

We stared at each other for a long moment until I finally broke the silence.

"How about this: I won't tell my dad on one condition—you tell me the whole truth. What's wrong with you. Why you are the way you are. I just want to understand."

He took a deep breath, weighing the options. "Okay," he agreed.

"No attitude, and no sarcasm."

"Oh, well, *that*..." he blutred sarcastically. I gave him a stink-eye, and he stopped himself. "Fine. Deal," he mumbled.

34. Quinn

WE WALKED ALONG THE cobblestone streets, moving in and out of patches of shimmer and shadow that painted the sidewalk. Puffy clouds hurried across the sky above us, revealing tantalizing glimpses of the winter sun.

She cautiously prodded my arm with her finger. "So can you feel that?"

"Yeah. I can tell that you're touching me, it's just that if you stuck a fork in my arm it would feel pretty much the same."

"What is it?"

I mumbled, "Some stupid thing, ana-something…"

"You mean you don't know what it's *called*?"

I rushed my revised answer, quick, clinical, and flat. "Congenital analgesia. It's a neurological condition, pretty rare. I can't feel pain, can't distinguish hot and cold. Most people who have what I have die before they grow up."

"Why?"

"When you feel something, you deal with it. It's the things you *don't* feel that come around and bite you in the ass."

"What do you mean?"

"Think about it," I snapped.

"You said no attitude," she said.

"No, *you* said no attitude."

Her glare was like a slap. I took a breath and tried again, like a kid getting back on the bike. "Imagine if your appendix burst but it didn't hurt so you never knew. If there was no alarm to tell you that you just broke your ankle, or had bent something too far and torn ligaments—or that the pan you picked up in the kitchen had actually just come out of the oven. Burns. Infections. Gangrene. Necrosis."

"Yeah, okay…I get it," she said.

We kept walking. The wind was picking up, and Reese pulled her little white cardigan around her body tighter, having walked out of the shop without a coat. I wished I could've given her mine, but I hadn't brought one either.

"Why didn't you tell me this before?" she asked. "This is major."

I coughed up a laugh. "It's not something I really announce to people. If no one really knows what my deal is, I get this kind of weird respect and people leave me alone. If I tell them, they get freaked out, or worse, they feel sorry for me."

"Donny said you were only a year ahead of me at Central, but I don't remember you at all."

"I didn't really…*go* too much. Or, well, at all."

"What do you mean? No one made you go to school?"

"Nah. I've always been able to do pretty much what I want. They probably figured why hassle me, I'll never have a real life so why do I have to learn calculus?"

"Why does *anyone* have to learn calculus? Your dad didn't care?"

I shook my head. "He didn't give a shit."

"And your mom left when you were five?" I nodded. "Do you remember her?" she asked. But I didn't answer because my attention had been hijacked by the sight of a woman stopped on the sidewalk, putting a woolly sweater over the head of her little boy. "It's okay, you don't have to talk about it," she said.

My mother had always tugged the opening of my shirt over my head so hard. I remembered looking up, trying to find her face as my oversized toddler head popped through the neck hole, trying to reconnect, but she was always already hunting around for my socks, my jacket, her gin and tonic.

"I don't really remember her very well. Mostly just what I've seen of her in photos or from what other people told me about her," I stammered to Reese.

One time, she had handed me a set of keys to keep me busy while she finished dressing me, and as she bent to put my socks on, I smacked her in the head with them, just because that's what kids do sometimes. Reflexively, she slapped me back, which just made me giggle. Thinking it was a game, I hit her with the keys again. So she picked me up without saying a word and dumped me—still half-dressed—behind a baby gate and closed herself in her room. I hadn't thought of that in a long time.

"She was kind of a nervous person, and I guess I was hard to deal with, so that's why she left," I said.

I remembered staring at that closed bedroom door through the wooden slats of the gate, bored, confused, and alone. I didn't remember if I had cried or not.

"And you think she left because of you?" asked Reese. "That's terrible. And I'm sure it's not true."

I suddenly realized I had been talking out loud. Deflect, repel, discourage. "Yeah, well, my mom didn't exactly...leave. She killed herself."

"Sometimes people leave no matter what you do."

"Did you hear what I said? She didn't walk out. She cut up her wrists and bled to death in the bathtub."

"Yes, I heard you."

We walked silently for a while.

"Thanks for telling me," said Reese quietly.

"You're blackmailing me, I didn't have a choice."

"Yeah. You did."

I glanced behind us and saw the Black Dog following from a distance. I felt that churning feeling in my gut.

"I want to take you somewhere and show you something, is that okay?" asked Reese.

"Yeah, yeah, sure," I said, distracted by the dog.

Above us, the clouds were thickening.

35. Caitlin

"**H**EY BABE, I'M UNDER the sink, can you hang on?"

"I'll just call you back—"

"No, no, hang on—"

Before she could protest, Caitlin heard the rustle of Will's T-shirt against his phone, she knew he'd put the phone down on his chest, a habit of his that drove her nuts. She sighed and went into the stall in the nurses lounge, phone to her ear, peeing while she waited for him to come back on the line.

She pictured him lying under the sink, repairing a leaky pipe in the firehouse kitchen, with the lower half of his six-foot frame stretched out across the cracked tile floor.

He had been promising to fix the dripping faucet in the upstairs bathroom at home, too, but he never seemed to remember. Too often lately it seemed like her only conversations with Will were "you do this," "I'll take care of that"—they hardly ever talked about anything other than how to just get through the day. It hadn't always been like that. She thought about the day she had met him, in the very same kitchen where they now ate breakfast and bickered about who hadn't done the laundry. He had just transferred to the firehouse, his first real, full-time firefighter job, and Dad had been impressed by his enthusiasm and willingness to do all the dumb, dirty jobs that no one else wanted to do. Dad loved to tell the story of how Will had jumped right in, scrubbing the pans after Jimmy had made his famous—and pain-in-the-ass to clean up after—firehouse ribs.

He brought Will home for dinner one night about two months after he'd started, and Caitlin had made a roast chicken and cornbread. Will later told her he was impressed she'd made such a grown-up meal. She was the most grown-up twenty-year-old he'd ever seen, he'd said, nearly a nurse already while her friends were all still out partying it up—but he thought she was funny, and dead gorgeous with a combination of light eyes and dark hair that he said slayed him at first sight. She'd loved how he listened to her like she was fascinating, how when he asked her about nursing school, it really seemed like he wanted to know. He had been surprised to meet Quinn that night— because apparently Dad had never mentioned him to Will. Quinn did his part to stay invisible by eating with hardly a word and disappearing down into his room before she could even take out the coffee cake she'd made for dessert. Dad acted more "fatherly" toward Will than toward his own son, which made Caitlin feel a little uncomfortable, though she knew it wasn't Will's fault. Dad scarfed his cake, and excused himself to catch the end of the BC football game with some chummy slaps on Will's muscled shoulder, leaving the two of them to finish their coffee together in the kitchen. Before she'd even poured Will a second cup, she knew she wanted to kiss him.

That was in March. She found out she was pregnant by October and they married in December, just the two of them at city hall on the day after Christmas because that was when their days off of work and school coincided. That felt like a lot longer than five years ago, she thought, and wondered if that was a good or a bad thing.

She flushed the toilet and slid open the stall lock, balancing the phone precariously between her ear and shoulder as she washed her hands, drying them on a burlap-y paper towel. She reached her still-moist right hand into her pocket, feeling the wadded up napkin she had stowed in there, but before she could pull it out, another nurse, in teddy bear scrubs—pediatrics—emerged from a stall and stood impatiently behind Caitlin, waiting for her to yield the single sink.

She left the bathroom, thinking about how Will felt he had been so incredibly patient, living in a house with her father and brother, putting up with her family's crap since they had gotten married—since before, really. But he wasn't that patient anymore, and he didn't have to say it, she could just feel his opinion radiating out at her whenever she got close, like a sun lamp without an off switch: Quinn wasn't getting his act together, he was getting worse, and Will thought he would be better off living somewhere else. The house felt emptier now without Dad, sick and angry as he had been for so long. And she knew Will missed him. But she didn't think he'd miss Quinn.

As Dad had gotten worse and worse, Will had gotten more vocal about what he wanted. And they'd had a couple of exhausting conversations where he'd told her what he really thought. That Quinn pulled everyone into his orbit and no one was better off for it. That in the time since Will had been with Caitlin, he thought she just seemed more and more flattened by life. That he wanted his family back. Wanted them to be a family for the first time, really—not just a satellite of another, more messed-up family. Winnie was already four, and he didn't want to have kids that were too far apart, it was time for another, this time on purpose, a boy maybe, and then they could be done. He'd put up with a lot, and let Caitlin handle things the way she wanted, but now it was time to steer this ship in a different direction. She didn't necessarily think he was wrong, but also resented that he seemed to be forcing her to choose between him and Quinn. So now she just bought time by avoiding any real conversations.

"Hey, babe." Will came back on the line.

"My shift's over and I'm gonna stop at the store on the way home. What do you want for dinner?" asked Caitlin, grabbing her purse from her locker and throwing her coat on over her scrubs.

"Forgot to tell you, I have a softball game tonight. I was gonna take Winnie—I told her she could be the bat girl."

"Oh. I'll just make something for me and Quinn then."

"How's his job search going?"

"I think he's waiting to hear on some things."

"I bet he's not even looking."

She wished he could see her face, so she could give him a glare. "People can change, Will."

"Uh-huh," he said, dubious.

"See you at home." Annoyed, she hung up without waiting for his goodbye. She shouldered open the door into the lounge bathroom again, checked the stalls to be sure she was alone this time before digging the wadded-up napkin out of her pocket. She opened it to reveal the two remaining stolen Vicodins. White and oval and gorgeous. It was becoming a thing, between her and the pills, more than just some fun friends-with-benefits arrangement—it was becoming a real relationship. She'd always been able to dip in and out, to take "as needed," but she had to admit she was starting to need it a lot more. Will didn't know, she was almost positive, but Quinn had noticed the fluctuations, the cycle of temptation and quitting, the crinkly white paper bags that she regularly brought home from the pharmacy for their father even though he rejected the pills more often than he took them.

Quinn wasn't an addict, but he thought like one, he acted like one, she thought—and it took one to recognize one. Just like an addict, he was constantly at war with self-destruction, dragging the family into his drama. Everyone telling him not to do it. Him knowing logically that it wasn't good for him, but unable to resist its pull, addicted to its ability to fend off others, to fend off life. She thought people did things that were bad for them if doing it seemed to solve a problem that felt worse than the new ones it caused. She took pain pills to solve the problem of the stress and anxiety of the rest of her life. She suspected that Quinn had discovered a long time ago that the things he did to damage his body helped keep others away, helped him to match his emotional state to his physical state. *Disconnected, untouchable, pain-free.* As she let herself look past how mad she almost always was at him in order to see it this way, she felt herself starting to cry. Not just because she felt sad for him, though there was definitely that too, but because she was jealous. She wished she had the luxury of shutting herself down like that for more than a couple of hours at a time.

She looked down at the pills again, nestled so cozily in the paper towel. She shook them into her other hand, slowly closed her fist around them—then flung them into the toilet and flushed them quickly, before she could have a chance to argue with herself. *People could change,* she thought, she had to believe they could.

36. Quinn

SHE LED ME ALONG a narrow cobblestone alley that I'd never walked down. I thought I knew every street in this neighborhood, but I'd never noticed this one. The alley opened up into a small grassy square in front of a tiny but well-preserved old stone church, nearly hidden by the surrounding buildings. I had seen the backside of the church from the main street, but it never occurred to me that of course there would be another way in. Coming upon this secret entrance and garden in my own neighborhood was like magically finding a totally new extra room in my house. We sat on a bench facing the front entrance of the church. Nearby, two little boys played catch in the little park, under the watchful eye of their mother.

"Isn't this place amazing?" Reese asked me. "Hardly anyone seems to know about it."

I noticed a life-sized figure carved into the façade of the church, one of those sort of flattened sculptures that are nearly flush with the wall. I thought it was Jesus, but then thought it was weird that he was tied to a tree instead of a cross. He had arrows stuck into his body, sticking out at all angles, and his eyes were turned up to the sky, looking for help. He had a hipster goatee. Groovy Jesus.

"That's Saint Sebastian." She'd noticed me staring. "Patron saint of archers and soldiers."

"Archers? That's warped."

She shrugged.

The little boys' ball flew wild and rolled across the gravel path toward our bench. I kicked it back to them.

Reese reached into her pocket and pulled out a wrinkled photo. She put it on her thigh and gently smoothed it out. It looked like a Sears studio portrait, or a school photo of your favorite third grade teacher. The woman in it had fluffy blonde hair, a guitar and a huge, warm smile. I could tell Reese wanted me to look at it closely, to ask her questions about it, but I just couldn't really. My stomach felt mushy.

"That's my mom," she said anyway. "I always keep her in my pocket. I used to come here with her when I was a little girl. She wanted to be a country singer."

"An Italian country singer from Boston?"

"I know, I know, that's what everyone said. But she frosted her hair and everything, she looked really authentic."

"Let me guess, she changed her name to Reba McEntire and you haven't heard from her since?"

"No. She never really got to Nashville. She died when I was ten. Brain cancer."

I nodded, not really sure what she wanted me to say. I tried to think what a normal person would say but came up blank.

"It was pretty awful. She just kind of slowly… faded, until it wasn't her anymore. And then it took another couple of months for her body to follow. I took care of her while she was sick and did all the cooking and cleaning and stuff at home."

"When you were ten?"

"Yeah. I was always like this—sick moms, stray cats, my dad. No one ever took care of me. I always felt kind of like I raised myself."

"Yeah. Me too."

She slipped the photo quietly back into her pocket. We just sat there for a while, watching the little boys throw the ball back and forth.

"Tell me about your drawings," she finally said. I was hoping she would've maybe forgotten about them.

"It's just a story I've been working on. I don't want to talk about it, it's dumb."

"It's not dumb."

"It's just...private. It's not finished, I don't even know the end."

"You don't know what happens?"

"No. That's kind of the problem." I sighed. The only way she was going to remotely get what I was talking about was if I showed her one or two, so I pulled a couple of drawings out of my bag. "When I started, it was pretty clear that the Shadow Man—"

"The big guy?"

"Yeah—that *he* was the hero, saving the world by hunting this Demon Boy, this monster child. But then I started to see the kid differently—you know, maybe he's just doing what he can in a world where everyone's against him. He's just trying to *live*. So now the Shadow Man seems more like the villain of the story, and I'm totally confused. I don't know who should win in the end. What do you think?"

"I think they're beautiful."

Oh man, she thought I was fishing for complements. "No, I mean about the ending. I've *got* to finish it—it's really messing with my head."

She just shrugged. "It's your choice. You know, I was thinking about that thing you said last night. The point of being alive? It's this." She pointed to my drawings. "Stuff like this can be a reason to be alive, a way to connect with other people. But only if you share it." She must've had the same nutjob art teacher as me. Art falling in the forest and no one hearing it, and all that.

"I don't really want to show it," I stressed, "It's just for me."

"What's the worst thing that could happen if you showed it? Someone doesn't like it? It's a risk. But life is pointless without risks."

I grabbed the drawings from her hand and shoved them back in my bag. "I just don't like to show them."

I must've managed to convey how not interested I was in talking about it, because she finally dropped it. She stood up abruptly and said, "It's getting cold. You wanna go inside?"

"Not really. Not really a church kind of guy."

"Come on, its beautiful." She pulled me to my feet and I was so relieved to be off the subject of the drawings that I went along.

The little boys' ball flew off course and lobbed straight at me. I instinctively put my right hand up to catch it—the bad one. With no cast supporting it, the wrist just flopped like a noodle and I dropped the ball. Quick, so no one would notice, I grabbed the ball with the other hand and pulled my sleeve down over the bad wrist to hide it—but Reese got a glimpse of how swollen and bruised it was.

"What happened?" she asked, with that same combination of fear and concern that Caitlin always had when she confronted me with that question.

"Nothing."

"It doesn't look very good. You should probably have a doctor check that out."

"I did. I mean, I will. It's not a big deal, it's nothing."

Weirdly, she laughed. "See? There I go. You don't need me telling you to look after it, but I do." Good, she made it about her. Deflect.

"Hey, give me my ball back!" Little kid was irate.

When I glanced over at the kid, what I saw standing there was the damn Demon Boy. It was daytime. This couldn't be. And seeing him now, he looked a little less like a drawing than before, and a little more like a real five-year-old boy, sort of a shimmering hybrid creature. From certain angles, he looked a whole lot like five-year-old me. Jesus, I was really losing it.

Demon Boy looked at me. "Please?"

Reese was ahead of me, starting up the church steps. "Give him his ball back. Let's go in." I tossed the ball back to the little kid. Demon Boy was gone.

"Thanks," the kid said sullenly, prompted by his mother.

I slowly followed Reese up the stairs, checking over my shoulder at the kid, who remained Demon Boy–free…

"I just thought, with your dad and all…" she said, "This place always makes me feel better when I'm really missing my mom."

Seriously? No thanks. "There's nothing for me to feel better about. I'm fine."

"I know. I just thought…never mind."

"There's nothing to miss—neither of my parents are around anymore—that's just the reality," I said. "All that other shit is just feeling sorry for yourself."

"Okay, okay. Forget it. I just want you to see the inside." She pulled on the iron door handle. As the massive wood door slowly swung open, I saw a familiar shape standing just inside the church door. The imposing silhouette of Shadow Man, staring straight at me.

"*Give him to me,*" he demanded in that low, seeping voice. I just wanted to run.

"I... I should go," I stuttered.

"What's wrong?" asked Reese.

"Nothing. I'll see you later. I'll see you at work."

"Quinn, wait."

So antsy. Had to go. "What?"

"I don't know if it really is a good idea for you to work in the shop... Because of, you know, your condition," she said quietly.

I just exploded at her. "We had a deal! You said you wouldn't tell if I explained it all to you."

"I just think maybe it's not the best idea..."

"Fine, then, I'll quit. You obviously have your own reasons why you don't want me to stay."

"No, that's not why..."

"I was going to quit anyway—I was just staying until I finished my drawings and then I was planning on leaving for good. So, I'll go back and tell your dad that I quit right now. Hey, thanks for everything. Have a nice life."

Her face crunched up with confusion, but I tore off before she could say anything else. I saw the Black Dog following me from a distance. He sure had a way of finding me.

✦

I STOOD, COLLAR UP against the wind, at a street corner about halfway back to the butcher shop. The wait for the light to change was endless. The passing cars left time-lapse ribbons of light in the gray gloom. My guts felt slushy. I just wanted to be home in my room, though the safety of my room usually meant the safety of drawing, and I couldn't draw. I knocked my fist impatiently against the lamppost, counting the seconds til I could cross. The knocking got harder and faster and I just let loose with a big punch to the metal in an effort to discharge the static in my brain—realizing after the fact that I'd done it with my bad hand. The light finally changed and I ran the rest of the way there.

37. Quinn

BURST IN THE FRONT door of the butcher shop, just wanting to quit and get it over with. A small mob of customers was shuffling around impatiently on the black and white tile and Donny and his father were both busy behind the counter.

"Quinn, where have you been?! And where is Reese?" Mr. R shouted.

"I'm sorry, Mr. Raffallo, but I need to talk to you."

"Well, I need to talk to you too."

My eyes darted to Donny, wondering if he'd already told his father, but he wouldn't meet my gaze.

I plunged ahead with my resignation. "Uh…I don't know what Donny or Reese might've told you, but effective immediately, I'm afraid I have to—"

"Effective immediately, I need you to slice up five pounds of lamb chops and deliver them to Mrs. Soto on Bennett Street. I promised she'd have them by five. Hurry."

"But…"

"Just do it."

He didn't know.

"Okay, but when I get back from that I need to talk to you." I said, coming around to join him behind the counter.

He put an arm around my shoulder. "You want a raise already? We'll talk."

He practically pushed me into the back room, hooking a clean apron off a pile with a sausage-y finger and shoving it into my hands. None of this was his fault. He was a nice guy and he was in a jam so I figured I should go help him out before quitting.

✠

I NEEDED TO SAW some lamb chops off a huge rack of ribs, and the knife felt as wrong as a pencil did in my left hand, so I tried to use my dominant-but-in-bad-shape right hand. It was pretty floppy but I tried to make up for that by muscling through, working quickly, aggressively. Reese appeared in the doorway, looking baffled.

"I thought you were quitting."

I kept working. "I am. I'm just doing a favor for your dad."

"Are you sure that's a good idea…?"

"It's just this one thing."

"Okay… I have to go help them up front, but I uh, just wanted to say I really enjoyed talking to you today."

"Yeah, it was all right."

"I'm sorry if I brought up a sensitive subject, you know, about your parents."

She caught my eyes for a long moment, like she was looking for a way in, a way to understand, to see me. I found that I couldn't really look away and I felt naked. It was kind of awkward, but not totally unpleasant, because I didn't feel any criticism in her stare, just curiosity.

Her eyes drifted down to my hands, which were sawing away at the chops, and I saw her expression change, in slow motion, from calm to panic.

"Stop!" She dashed forward.

With time slowed into thin, dissectible slices, I coolly looked down and registered first the fountain of red arterial blood and the interesting pattern it was making on the table in front of me. Then, I noted the fact that this blood was a brighter hue than the blood from the meat I was cutting. That meant it was mine. I looked closer and saw where the sharp butchering knife had wedged smoothly and deeply into the tender web between the thumb and forefinger of my left and formerly-good hand.

By now, Reese had reached me and grabbed the knife away. It clattered to the floor and, unblocked by the stainless steel blade, more of my blood flowed onto the stainless steel table, mixing with the lamb's blood.

I glanced up to see Donny looking on from the doorway. He turned away and moved out of sight.

Reese reached for a white dish towel. "Here, wrap it in this."

She laid it out on the table and I rested my bloody hand on it. As she bound me up in the towel, I saw Mr. R's face through the doorway, his expression serious as Donny spoke to him up at the front counter. When Donny finished talking, Mr. R came into the back room. My hand was tightly wrapped, but the blood was already starting to leach through the white cloth.

"Donny tells me you hurt yourself—is it bad?" Mr. R asked me.

"No, no, I think it'll be fine."

"Good." He shifted his weight uncomfortably. "Quinn, you are a good employee for me so far, you know that."

"Thank you," I said, uncertain.

"Donny says that you…you haven't told me the whole truth. He says there is a medical condition, that you can't tell when you have hurt yourself."

Reese tried to break in, "Daddy, he—"

"You see, I *knew* there was something wrong with him from the start!" Donny yelped from the doorway. He was hopping up and down on the balls of his toes, agitated, like he was releasing all the pent-up energy he had bottled up in his body by keeping my secret from his father all day.

"Donny—" warned his father.

"Sir, that's true. I'm sorry I didn't tell you, but—"

"Quinn, I can't have you working here. For your own good. I'm sorry."

"I understand." There wasn't much else I could say.

He gestured to my wrapped hand. "Let me see."

I unwrapped the towel and the cut flapped and pulsed viciously.

"Shit," I blurted. Had to respect that little bastard's impressive and bloody display.

Mr. R was alarmed. "This is a hospital cut—Reese, go with him to the emergency room." He took some money from the register and pushed it into her hand, herding us out the front door, past the gaping customers. "Here, go, get a taxi down on the corner—go, go!"

⁂

AS I STEPPED OUT onto the sidewalk, the panic hit me like a blast from a cold hose. Not because of my bleeding hand, but because I knew that if I set foot in the hospital, Caitlin would hear about it, and the jig would be up.

"Shit, shit, shit, shit…" I ducked into the recessed doorway of a closed shop and paced a tiny circle. My body was jittering, bad.

"What are you doing? We need to go!" Reese stared at me.

"Just stay away from me. I can't go to the hospital."

'What are you talking about?"

"My sister works there—she can't find out about this."

"Why?"

"Just trust me, she can't know. This will really hurt her." She reached out to touch my shoulder and I freaked. "Get away from me!"

"Why?"

"I fucking hurt people."

"*You're* hurt."

"That's the *least* of my problems right now."

"What do you mean?"

I crouched down in the doorway, huddling against the closed shop's door. "I need to leave. I shouldn't even be here— it's a bad joke, a mistake. I should just go."

"And go where?"

"That's the thing!" My voice went high into panic register. I was losing my shit. Me taking a job in a butcher shop had been like a private joke between me and the universe, but now it occurred to me that maybe Caitlin had been right. I *was* reckless, deliberately self-destructive, killing myself slowly. I knew I would rather kill myself quickly than go to that place she'd taken me to—but I'd been stupid. I'd created a situation that made it so I'd have to do that sooner than I'd been planning and there were still things I needed to do. I hadn't finished the story.

"I'm not ready," I howled.

"Hey hey hey, it's okay, shhhh…" she murmured. She knelt down and gently cupped her hands around my towel-wrapped hand. "You need help."

"No, I don't."

"I want to help you."

"How?"

She reached out and took my other hand, helped me to my feet and pulled me wordlessly down the sidewalk. I followed like a blind dog on a leash.

38. Reese

A MAGICAL HALF-LIGHT PERMEATED THE church. Dusty shafts of saturated color drifted effortlessly from the stained glass that ringed the upper walls. I sat with Quinn in a side chapel, blanketed in a rich pink twilight that poured in through a high window. This was my favorite place in the world, but it felt a little weird to be sharing it with him under these circumstances. Benevolent saints surrounded us on all sides, their figures frozen in the panes above, but other than us the only other living being in the church was a tiny, stooped old woman, praying, still and silent, in a front pew.

I pulled a little sewing kit out of a drugstore bag, slid the needle free and twisted its tip over the flame of a votive candle to sterilize it. Five different colored bands of thread were wrapped tightly around the little finger of cardboard—I decisively chose the red, unwound a two-foot piece, knotted one end and threaded the other through the needle's eye. I hadn't been in that many genuine emergency situations in my life, and it felt important to try to be one of those people who could be "good in a crisis."

"Hold still." I started stitching up his wound. The delicate needle ducked neatly in and out of his skin, tugging the two sides closer and closer together and slowing the flow of blood. As I worked, with my head bent deeply over Quinn's hand, I noticed he wasn't looking at what I was doing—he was looking at the side of my face, really calmly, and it made me feel nervous.

"Oh, look, you're getting it all over your shirt," I fussed, futilely trying to push his sleeve up and away from the blood that was still trickling spindly red branches down his hand.

"Hold on." He twisted a quarter turn away from me and slipped his shirt up and over his head.

"Oh my God," I breathed to myself. There, across Quinn's entire back, was a gorgeous, fearsome tattoo. It was an intricate, almost medieval-looking picture—done in the same painterly style as his drawings, with the same characters—it showed the Shadow Man carrying the Demon child inside a giant domed cage with one hand and holding off the Black Dog with the other.

I just stared at it, amazed by the scale, the statement, the commitment. It said more about his relationship to his artwork than he could probably ever have said with words, and I wanted to somehow tell him that I could see that, but I knew I would start to cry if I did, so instead I just said, "It's beautiful."

"Thanks," he said, kind of self-consciously, and then I knew for sure that the tattoo did mean all those things to him, and it embarrassed him to see me recognizing that.

"I've thought about getting one," I said, trying to act all casual.

"Oh yeah?"

"Just a little one—but I was always afraid it would hurt."

"Well…"

"But the main reason I didn't is that I couldn't imagine what I could get that would be meaningful for my entire life. What if I got older and I hated it?"

"Yeah, well, I was never supposed to get older."

I couldn't stop looking at it. "It looks just like your drawings."

"Yeah, they're all from dreams I have. This was one I had a lot when I was a kid. A lot. Once I got the tattoo, though, I stopped having the dream. Isn't that weird?"

"Yeah."

"Same thing used to happen with my drawings—I had to draw it to stop dreaming it—but lately I haven't been able to draw, you know, because of my wrist."

"So what happens?"

"The dreams have gotten, well…more *vivid*." It seemed like he was about to tell me something more, but then thought better of it.

My eyes still travelled over his tattoo, studying, searching. I traced my finger slowly over the part of the image with the caged boy. Against my will, my eyes welled up, and my nose got a little sniffly.

"He looks so scared," I said super quietly.

Quinn turned around and touched my face, leaking blood on me. "Oh, God, I'm sorry about that," he said, wiping off my cheek with his balled-up shirt.

"It's okay. No, really, it's okay," I said. It seemed like he might kiss me or something and my brain started buzzing nervously.

And right at that moment, the little old lady in the front pew slowly rose and started shuffling her way slowly, hunchingly down the center aisle toward the rear door. She took a small step, then matched it with the other foot. Small step and match, small step and match, like a slowed-down, reversed mirror of her wedding march likely down this same aisle fifty or sixty years earlier. We both turned and watched her go for the longest time.

And then, when we turned back to each other, I just did it. I kissed him.

It felt perfect, powerful, and mercifully uncomplicated.

39. Quinn

We walked back toward our neighborhood, smiling kind of secretly to ourselves but not saying much. My senses felt supercharged. I was aware of every little brush of her sweater against my arm. I heard her soft breathing like it was amplified, and saw the clear outlines of every exhale in the chilly dusk air. It was getting darker and colder with every step we took, but my heart was beating fast and strong and I felt warmed from the inside, a walking wood stove.

When a kid came barreling down the sidewalk on his bike, I curled my arm around her shoulder and pulled her toward me for a moment until he had passed. I was surprised at my protectiveness; it felt wobbly, like a word you had only seen in a book and were trying out loud for the first time, unsure that you were pronouncing it correctly. But it also felt right and I liked it. Little sprouts of optimism were emerging and it seemed suddenly like things might possibly work out okay.

⁂

It was dark by the time we reached my street, where the white holiday lights in the trees were glistening like tears. I'd wanted to walk her to her house first, but she'd rejected that idea, for obvious reasons. We stopped at the bottom of my front steps and I suddenly felt all awkward, like I wasn't sure what to say.

"So...I'll see you later?" I ventured.

"Yeah," she nodded.

After a weird pause that made us both laugh half-nervously, she gave me a quick kiss on the cheek and headed off down the sidewalk. I watched her for a moment, then walked lightly up the stairs and into the house, an unnameable weight lifted.

40. Caitlin

AITLIN WAS AT THE stove, making dinner. Quinn hummed as he entered the kitchen, hands in his pockets, and collapsed into one of the plastic aqua chairs at the table. She was glad that he didn't look at her closely enough to notice that she was pale and shaky.

"Where have you been?" she asked, stirring the spaghetti sauce.

"Oh, Cait, I can't even begin to explain," he sighed, relaxed and oddly good-natured.

"How about you try?" She turned around to see him quietly spacing out, staring pleasantly at the wall. "What's going on? Is something wrong?"

"I don't know. I feel…different."

"Different how?"

"Just tired, I guess."

"I'm not feeling so well either. Must be going around."

She turned back to stir the pot on the stove, more to avoid eye contact while she said something difficult than because it needed her attention.

"You know… I just wanted to let you know how proud I am that you've really made an effort to find a job. I…I'm also really trying to pull it together, you know? I realize I haven't always been… Well, it's a new start for us, for the family, and I feel like you're seeing it that way too, and I just wanted to say I appreciate that. Did you get the job you were waiting on?"

He didn't reply, and she wondered if she'd said something wrong. Maybe it was a sore issue. "Well I'm sure you'll hear soon, right?"

She turned to him for a response and saw him slumped back in his chair—was he sleeping? Jesus, no, he was unconscious. She noticed that the entire left side of his jacket and his left pant leg was wet. His left hand fell from his jacket pocket and dangled, limp, dripping blood onto the pocked linoleum floor. Her heart racing, she picked up his hand and examined the bloody wound, gaping open where the homemade stitches had ripped free.

41. Reese

HEADED HOME, BACK ALONG the same route Quinn and I had just walked, coming from the church.

Snowflakes silently cartwheeled from the sky and the cold night air felt new and clean on my face. I skied two fingers along a flat metal railing as I walked, slaloming a trail through the powder. I spun around, looking up at the flakes sifting through the forks of the naked trees. They caught on my eyelashes and melted against my flushed cheeks. One of my heels skidded on something slippery and I nearly fell. When I looked down to see what it was, I saw freshly-fallen snowflakes melting into a crimson trail of drops, smudges and tiny puddles, leading back toward Quinn's house. Confused, I stared at them for a moment.

An ambulance siren carved the air, growing louder and louder, preceding its source. The ambulance rocketed down the street, past me, heading in the direction of Quinn's house. I put the trail and the ambulance together and took off running, back to him.

42. Quinn

O F ALL THE EMERGENCY room cubicles I've sat in in my life, which is a hell of a lot, this was the worst. Not because of what had happened to my body—I'd just lost too much blood without realizing it and passed out, not that big a deal— but because of the grilling I was receiving from Caitlin as the ER doc silently re-stitched the cut on my left hand.

"Cait, things are changing, they're different. They're better," I insisted, pushing my right hand, the one with the messed-up wrist, further into my pocket so the doc—a new young one I'd never seen before—wouldn't notice it and insist on putting a hard cast on it.

"*This* is not *better*," Caitlin said, pointing to my new stitches, "and I can't watch you twenty-four seven."

"You're not responsible for me."

"Apparently, neither are you. Look at yourself. You could just as easily have cut off your hand—a butcher shop? A *butcher shop* for Chrissakes? What were you thinking?"

"I don't know."

"And you *lied* to me."

"I didn't lie. I was just...non-specific."

"Stop it. You backed me into a corner and now I have no choice."

"You can't just decide. You said yourself only a shrink can make me go."

"At this point, I think that's really just a formality. It's not going to be hard to show a pattern of 'suicidal behavior.'"

Holy freakin' moly she was serious. "Can we at least talk about this?"

"There's nothing to talk about. The decision is out of my hands."

She had never sounded like this before—she meant it and there was no opening I could see, no argument I could make, no weak spot to exploit. I looked around helplessly for a way out. I saw Cait's purse slumped on a baby blue plastic chair.

✖

CAIT AND I, WITH my newly-bandaged left hand, walked toward the exit doors. Reese, who had been forced to wait out in the reception area, came running down the corridor after us.

"Quinn, wait," she yelled. But I didn't want to talk to her. Not now. I didn't want to think about the fact that I had to abandon whatever that brief, incandescent thing had been between us. I just couldn't live in that place Caitlin was sending me, and I didn't see any other option but to go back to my original plan: to exit the world. I put my tunnel vision on and walked faster, ignoring Reese.

Caitlin stopped, rooting around in her purse. "Shit. I must've left my keys in there, I'll be right back," she said, marching back to the treatment area. I pulled her car keys from my pocket, stomped on the pressure pad to open the automatic doors, and hurried out into the parking garage. Reese followed me. Shit, she was going to screw this up.

"Can I talk to you?" she called after me.

"No." I reached the car and unlocked the door. She caught up and grabbed my jacket.

"Quinn…"

"I'm really sorry, I just, I gotta go."

"What's going on?"

"Please, come on—leave me alone."

I just wanted her to let me go, to step away so I could leave, and I pushed her, harder than I meant to, against the side of the car, trying to hold her there until I could get into the driver's door.

"You're hurting my arm!" she cried.

"Quinn!" Caitlin came booking out of the automatic doors toward us. Damn it.

I wrenched open the car door. Reese tried to hold my arm to stop me. Desperate to get out of there, I grabbed her and shoved her out of the way. The bad wrist bent weirdly back and there was a snapping sound but I didn't have time to think about that.

I jumped into the driver's seat and started the car, jammed it in reverse, and lurched backward out of the parking space, but then, just as I paused to put it in forward gear, Reese jerked open the left rear door and clambered into the back seat.

Caitlin was racing toward the car, screaming at me to stop, now twenty feet away, now ten feet away.

I peeled out.

✖

I DIDN'T REALLY KNOW how to drive. I mean I knew that the gas was on the right and the brake on the left, but aside from Will letting me fart around in a mall parking lot a couple of times for a laugh when I was fifteen, I'd never really operated a car. So it took some concentration to drive fast while trying to remember to watch out for stop lights and stuff like that. Not to mention my left hand was so packed with gauze that it was more like a giant thumbless paw than a useful, gripping extremity, and my right hand with the bad wrist was only slightly more able to maneuver the steering wheel, so precision driving was tough.

I immediately headed away from the traffic on the main streets, instead going down toward an industrial area near the waterfront. It also didn't help my concentration that Reese was awkwardly climbing from the back seat to the front.

"What are you doing?" she screamed at me.

"What are *you* fucking doing? Get out of the car."

I slowed the car down and leaned across and tried to open the passenger door, but she shoved me away, the car swerving left and right as we did. It was a pretty deserted area and there were hardly any cars, just the occasional slow-moving, smoke-belching semi.

"No. Tell me what's going on." She jammed her seatbelt into the buckle with a defiant click. She wasn't going anywhere.

"My sister's trying to send me away to some institution."

"Why?"

"Because of where I worked. Because you told her."

"But you're quitting."

"It doesn't matter."

"Well, how was I supposed to know that?"

I glanced in the rearview mirror and goddammit if I didn't see the Black Dog sitting in the back seat of the car, staring me right in the eye. I whipped my head around to look, but there was nothing back there. I sped up.

"I don't know what your sister said, but I'm sure she's only trying to help you," she said.

"It doesn't matter because I am *not* going to live in that place. I'm letting you out up ahead."

"So you can go where and do what?"

"Something I should have done a long time ago, okay?"

She grabbed my shoulder. "What are you talking about?"
I shrugged her hand off. "What do you care?"

"I care," she insisted.

"Well don't, it only ends badly."

"That's bullshit."

"Not in my family. My family isn't like yours, where everyone basically loves each other despite their funny little flaws. Where the biggest problem is 'awww, should Reese go off to college now or later?' 'Awww, which is more adorable, cinnamon sticks or puppy-dog tails?' In *my* family, bad shit happens, I hurt people, I screw up their lives and there isn't much I can do about that except stop living."

Reese sat quietly for a moment, digesting that. "And you don't think *that* will hurt your sister?"

"They've been expecting it for years. It would be a relief, probably."

"I think you're just scared," she said.

"Of *what*?"

"You put up this tough front—you 'don't care' if you die, it's for other people's good—all noble. You're so convinced that if people care about you, they're going to get hurt. Well, I think you're afraid if *you* care about *them*, you're the one that'll get hurt. And you'd rather die than feel that again."

"That's crap," I snapped.

"Oh no it isn't, I know all about it," she said. "After my mom died, I swore I'd never let myself love anybody that much ever again—so I could never get that hurt ever again."

I stared at her. I did know that feeling. I didn't want to think about it though. My right foot stiffened on the gas pedal and the car accelerated a bit more.

"But you know, that's just the cost of being alive," she continued. "You don't get any of the good stuff in life unless you risk the bad stuff."

One wheel of the car skittered onto the dirt shoulder and I jerked the car back onto the tarmac.

She kept going. "All that stuff you said to me about caring being a 'crutch,' or a 'weakness'—it's not. Remember, in the walk-in, when you asked me how we were different from some frozen side of beef? It's love, Quinn. Without that, we're just meat."

"Then I'm just meat," I insisted.

"No, you're not. Because if you were, it wouldn't matter if you were in or out of some institution, it wouldn't matter if you were alive or dead."

"It *doesn't* matter. I *don't* care."

"I don't believe you. And I think pretending you don't care is the most cowardly thing you could possibly do."

I felt like my chest might explode with anger and I just flew into attack mode.

"Don't talk to *me* about cowardly. About risk. You're the one who wants to stay at home in your safe little neighborhood and look after your dad—who'd be fine without you by the way."

She flinched. "What?"

I was still just winding up. We were really barreling along the waterfront now. To our right, through a guardrail and down a concrete embankment, was the edge of the harbor. To the left was a long line of warehouse loading docks.

"And what's with your stupid outfits, while we're at it? God forbid you might dress like yourself one day."

"You know, forget it," she said, reaching for her door handle.

"Maybe you'll be in a position to lecture me when you finally decide which personality is your own."

"Stop the car. I want you to let me out."

"Oh, you don't like it when it comes back at you?"

"Shut up, Quinn, at least I try, okay?"

"So do I—but no one seems to freakin' notice."

"But you don't. Seriously—you don't have anyone to blame but yourself if you get sent away—it's your own damn fault."

The dog in the back seat—the dog I knew wasn't there—started barking. And barking.

"Shut up! Shut the fuck up!" I yelled.

"Let me out!" She pulled the door handle and the passenger door swung wide open—I reached across, trying to get her to close it.

The damn dog wouldn't stop barking.

When I looked back up, I that saw an oncoming semi truck was coming toward us, slow and steady, arcing a wide right turn toward a loading bay—fully into our lane. It blasted its air horn and jolted to a stop.

I veered wide right, just skirting around the front end of the truck's massive cab. The back of the car fishtailed right, scraping the guardrail and kicking up a cloud of dust, the back right wheel flirting with the edge of the concrete embankment that sloped steeply into the water. Blinded by the dust, I jerked the car back to the left to get back on the road, but as we came out the other side of the cloud, I swear to Dog, I saw them. Shadow Man and Demon Boy were standing side by side in the middle of the road, looking right at me, and I was about to smash the car right into them both.

43. Quinn

I JAMMED MY FOOT DOWN on the brake.

Reese screamed.

The car screech-skidded to a stop right in front of Shadow Man and Demon Boy.

I reached for my door handle.

"What are you doing?" asked Reese.

"Go," I told her, "Seriously, go now—just walk away. Please."

"No," she said. "What's going on?"

I got out of the car, leaving my door open, and went over to them.

Shadow Man's arms were folded angrily across his chest and he puffed loudly and impatiently with each exhale, like a bull in a rodeo chute, ready to explode. A single deep word seeped coldly from him: "*Choose.*"

"Let me go," I said. "I have to go."

"*No*," he breathed, impatient, "*First you choose.*"

Demon Boy looked up at me, wide-eyed and petrified. He now looked almost entirely like a human child, with just a little pencil line quaver around the edges.

Behind me, the semi driver leaned out of his cab and yelled down to Reese, "You okay, Miss?"

"Yes...uh...I don't know," she called back, out the car window. "What's going on?" she yelled to me. "What are you doing?"

The semi driver shrugged, unlocked his brakes with a hiss and started the truck rolling forward to the warehouse again.

"Please don't kill me," pleaded Demon Boy. *"Please?"*

I looked back and forth between him and the Shadow Man. And then it happened so slow.

As the semi rumbled forward and completed its turn, clearing the roadway, a pick-up truck that had been speeding down the road zipped around its back end. As he swerved around the semi, the driver didn't expect to see a car stopped in the middle of the road, right in front of him. I heard the squealing brakes as he tried to slow and swerve around the car, and whipped my head around toward the noise, just as the pick-up clipped the open driver's side door, spinning the car around.

"No!" I turned to run toward the car, and my eyes locked with Reese's—still in the passenger seat, her face in shock—as the car spun, smashed through the guardrail and slid down the concrete embankment toward the water. The pick-up truck paused briefly as the driver, a big hulking guy with tiny pig eyes, registered what had happened, then sped forward again. I instinctively grabbed onto the back gate of the truck bed as he accelerated past me.

"Hey! Hey!" I screamed.

My legs flew out from under me and I dragged and bumped along for a few seconds before I lost my grip and went tumbling end over end along the asphalt. Up was sideways was down. I came to rest in a crumpled heap in the middle of the road as the pickup disappeared down the waterfront.

I tried to get up, but it wasn't happening. I'd done some damage somewhere and my legs wouldn't cooperate. I think I'd also hit my head pretty bad because I was so dizzy that I still wasn't sure which way was up. I slowly creeped on my elbows, army-crawl style, over to the edge of the embankment and saw the car resting on its side, passenger door down, drivers' door facing the sky, on the little concrete apron down at the bottom. The apron was just wide enough for one vehicle, and the car was inches from the water's edge, smoke pouring from the engine. I couldn't really see Reese, just a dark shape in the passenger seat, and I couldn't tell if she was moving or what was going on. Black smoke was everywhere, and when I tried to focus my eyes I thought I saw delicate flames licking around the edges of the hood. I tried to angle my body around so I could put my legs under the guardrail, maybe I could slide down the embankment, but I was fading in and out of consciousness, and it felt like it was taking me hours to move each foot.

A blur of motion crossed my half-closed eyes, and I opened them to see Demon Boy scrambling down the embankment toward the car. Flames were now dancing all around the front end of the car—the engine compartment and upper face of the car were on fire and it was spreading quickly. Demon Boy grabbed a fist-sized rock and hammered at the back window until it shattered. He dove through the window, and emerged moments later, through flames, dragging Reese with him. She was moving a little bit, definitely alive, trying to hold onto him. He pulled her about twenty feet away from the car, down the little concrete strip, then put her down gently onto the ground where she lay still, eyes closed, breathing hard. My own heart was racing, just watching them.

There was a small explosion from the car, just a pop, and the whole thing was suddenly engulfed in flames that twisted up toward the sky like vines, ten feet high.

I felt a cold draft and looked up; Shadow Man was standing behind me, expressionless, looking past me as I lay sprawled and useless at the top of the embankment. We both looked down at Demon Boy standing small but triumphant next to Reese, his chest heaving, trying to catch his breath.

Through the heat shimmer, the Boy looked right up at me, right into my eyes, as if to say, *"How about now?"*

And then everything went white and silent.

44. Quinn

S WIMMY IMAGES AND SMEARED colors came in and out of half focus.

Abstract sounds slowly became recognizable. Making some kind of sense of the constant squeak squeak of the nurses' shoes out in the hallway took up the better part of an afternoon, with some dream logic detours to alternate locales, like an abandoned house with a giant, swinging door, and a dark cave full of savage guinea pigs. That was exertion enough to plunge me back into unconsciousness.

Hours or days later, I unbuttoned one eyelid, lashes still crisped together, like a pair of spiders glued over my eyes. Through the left spider, a blurry landscape revealed itself. Machines, IV tubing, a mute television. A wall clock without a second hand that imperceptibly oozed its way forward in time. A white board on the far wall that said: "Your nurse's name is: Crystal. Today is: Friday ☺."

And at the foot of the bed, Caitlin. Sitting. Reading a book.

She hadn't noticed that I was awake. She checked her watch, got up, and started putting on her coat over her surgical greens.

"Why...you...?" I croaked. More than a few words got lost on the way from my brain to my mouth.

She startled a bit. "What?

"...Why...are you here?"

"You're in the hospital. You had an accident."

"No kidding. Why...are you here?"

"What do you mean?"

"I thought you'd just send. Guys with butterfly nets. To pick me up."

She reached over and put her hand to my forehead to check my temperature.

"How do you feel?"

"I don't know," I closed my eyes. "Tired. Where's Reese?"

"Down the hall. Her injuries…" She was reluctant to finish the sentence.

"Don't tell me. I don't want to hear."

"I can take you down to see her later if you want."

"I don't want to see her."

"Well, maybe when you're feeling up to it."

I raised my voice to a shouting whisper. "I don't want to see her."

"Okay, it's okay. Relax. She's not seeing anyone right now, and I don't think you should be either."

"I shouldn't have gotten out, shouldn't have left the door open…"

"Do you want something to eat? Soup? I can run down to the cafeteria for you, it should still be open…"

"It was my fault…"

My brain swirled with overlapping lines, like handfuls of charcoal pencils, filling in the empty space with black scrawled scribbles, until finally it went completely black.

45. Caitlin

"**I**T WASN'T YOUR FAULT, it was an accident..."

Caitlin wanted to impress this idea forcefully into Quinn's head, but he had already drifted back into a hazy sleep. It didn't seem particularly peaceful though. Caitlin sat on the bed next to him and stroked his forehead, trying to gently smooth out the furrows, but they were stubborn.

A nurse bustled in, erased Crystal's name off the white board with the pad of her thumb, and wrote in "Rhonda" in purple marker. She pulled a small bottle of liquid and a syringe out of her pocket and whirled around toward the bed. "Good evening, I'm Rhonda your new shift nurse. Are we ready for our morphine?" she chirped with professional cheer.

"He doesn't need it," said Caitlin.

Rhonda prickled. "Well, that's really the patient's decision."

"He doesn't need it—check his chart," she sighed.

Rhonda consulted the sheet of meds orders in her hand. "Says right here, every four hours, Ernie Rosenbaum, 323A."

Caitlin pointed to the number above Quinn's bed—332A.

Without missing a beat, the nurse bustled out the door and into the room across the hall. "Good evening, I'm Rhonda your new shift nurse. Are we ready for our morphine?"

Caitlin collected her things, took one last look at Quinn sleeping, and slipped out of the room. It was a relief to have him be under another roof, someone else's responsibility these last few days. She was acutely aware he might not ever be under her roof again. Obviously, it was a relief that no one had died. But she was glad it had been such a definitive event. She couldn't even argue with herself about it—he clearly needed more care and supervision than she could provide. But as she left the hospital and stepped out into the frosty night air, she felt a little bit uneasy that the die had been cast, a little bit guilty about feeling less frayed, less torn than she ever had.

46. Quinn

I GUESS I HAD BROKEN a few ribs, my right ankle, bruised some internal organs, had some nasty gravel abrasions on my hands and arms and chest, stuff like that, but my body didn't hurt. It just felt deeply, crushingly tired.

I really didn't want to go see Reese, it's hard to explain why—I mainly felt ashamed. Humiliated. I had hurt her just like I had hurt everyone else around me, and I guess I was afraid to see the proof. When I finally woke fully up, on the fourth day, all I wanted to do was get out of the hospital, just run. Get away from anyone I knew. I didn't want to hurt them more.

I had this idea that I could simply sneak out of the hospital and disappear. It took me about twenty minutes just to get myself up to a sitting position in the bed with my legs on the floor. Every time I moved a muscle, it felt like I had had the wind knocked out of me, and I needed to rest a minute until I could breathe again. When I finally tried to stand up, it was pretty obvious that I wasn't going to be walking much of anywhere. The cast on my ankle didn't bother me at all—but when I tried to get upright, my legs spaghettied all over the place. I think when you lay in bed without moving for a few days, your body doesn't like it too much. I wobbled and lurched the three steps over to the wheelchair that was parked against the wall. After a short rest, I was able to maneuver the thing slowly out the door, even though my arms were bandaged shoulder to wrist, like a mummy, and my bad wrist was now encased in an annoyingly stiff plaster cast.

It was the morning nurses' shift change, and there were a lot of people going this way and that, so no one seemed to notice me slowly wheeling down the corridor. I just kept my head down and crept along, hoping I was going in the direction of an elevator. When I looked up to see if I could spot an exit sign or something, I saw Reese's dad, Mr. R, sitting on a bench at the very end of the hallway, praying silently. His head suddenly popped up, like he'd sensed me looking at him, and stared right at me. His face was pink and puffy from crying. Neither of us moved.

Donny saw me and came run-walking down the hall, trying not to spill the two lidless paper cups of coffee in his fists. He gave both cups to his father, bent to whisper something to him, then came over to me. His face was pomegranate red. The veins on the sides of his neck were bulging—and I noticed his neck was somehow, bizarrely and amazingly, even wider than his head. Why hadn't I noticed that before? I knew it was an inappropriate thought at that moment, but there it was.

He stopped right in front of me, his shins brushing my toes, which were poking stupidly off the footrest of the wheelchair. He leaned forward to speak quietly and menacingly in my face. "If my father wasn't sitting here—swear to God—I'd bust your goddamned freak ass. Due to what you did, you have no business coming near my sister's room."

"I wasn't…"

"All because of your little Bonnie and Clark routine, she's lying in there all messed up with pins in her ankle and screws in her knee and God knows what else. They didn't even know if she was going to make it at first."

I was not up for this. I did a clumsy one-eighty and wheeled back the way I came, but he followed right behind me, getting louder and louder, yelling at the back of my head as I rolled myself down the hall. People stopped to stare.

"Do you understand me? She could have died. She could have died and it would have been on your head. Do you know what that would do to my father? Do you know?" By now he was flat out shouting. I just let the chair roll to a stop and sat there in the middle of the hallway. "Why don't you just *think* about that?" he added quietly, before turning and heading back to sit down with his father on the bench.

All I could do was sit there, frozen. I couldn't breathe. I couldn't move. I couldn't open my mouth to protest when a nurse came and wheeled me back into my room. Did it not occur to Donny that I *was* already thinking the exact same things he had just said to me, except ten times worse?

47. Quinn

S
O I HAD TO do it then, there.

As a fat man jumped up and down, wanting to solve the *Wheel of Fortune* puzzle on the blaring TV above my hospital bed, I moved methodically through the room, as best I could, looking for something I could use. Phone cord? Too short. Curtains? Too thick. Curtain rods? Too flimsy. I dragged my body into the bathroom and opened the mirrored medicine cabinet. Q-Tips, disposable toothbrush, no, no. A nail clipper. I took it. When I closed the cabinet, I saw, reflected in it, standing behind my shoulder, the Shadow Man. I could feel his cold breath on my neck. As always, he spoke without a mouth.

"So, does this mean I get the Boy?"

I hadn't come up with an ending for him, but now there wasn't time. "I don't care. Yes," I said to him.

"Thank you."

I left the bathroom and pulled the top sheet off the bed. I pulled the mummy bandages away from my hands so I could use them better and noticed the abrasions on my palms were sort of weepy and bubbly, which I thought was a little weird, but I dismissed it and forged on.

I used the nail clippers to clip a little notch into the edge of the bed sheet and then ripped a long strip off of it. I looked around for something to tie it to—decided on the ceiling-mounted television. I started rigging up a noose. Fat *Wheel of*

Fortune man failed to guess the phrase "Double Whammy" and the audience went "awwwww."

As I worked, the Shadow Man stalked around the room, hunting for the Demon Boy under the bed, behind doors. He opened the narrow closet—and there he was. Demon Boy was now completely human-looking, but still apparently had his pyrotechnic abilities—because he screamed a fireball and set the closet on fire as he rushed out, leading the Shadow Man on a crazed chase around the room. It was really distracting.

"Stop it! Can you please just wait until I'm done?" I shouted at them.

The battling pair—animated Shadow Man and human-seeming Demon Boy—stood still in a temporary truce. They watched in silence as I dragged a chair beneath the television, climbed slowly, awkwardly up onto it, hooked the sheet over the TV mount, tied it, and put my neck in the loop. The fabric felt smooth and cool.

I took a deep breath and then I did it.

I stepped off the chair.

I couldn't breathe.

The room slowly went red.

The main thing I remember about hanging there was the sound of the shrieking game show audience on the television. Nothing else happened for a long time.

Suddenly, the TV gave way with an ear-crunching sound, and I fell to the ground in a messy heap, gasping, the television and a large chunk of the ceiling smashing to bits all around me.

Silence. Drywall dust drifted, ghostly, through the air.

Then, the sound of a man laughing started to fill the room. It built hysterically and then turned into a terrible hacking cough. I looked up and saw my father, my damn dead father, in the room's formerly empty second bed.

"Jesus boy, fucking get it done already." Yep, that was him alright.

"What's so funny?" I wheezed, coughing out dust.

"It's a joke, a goddamn joke. You damage everyone around you—everyone but yourself. Fucking hilarious."

"Fuck you."

"Is that how you speak to your father?"

Doctor Silverman and a nurse came rushing into the room. "What was that noise?"

"Jesus, are you okay?"

The Shadow Man shushed Silverman for interrupting. The nurse tried to help me up off the floor but I shoved her away. Silverman whispered something to the nurse and she went running out the door. I turned back toward my dad—I knew the doc would think I was nuts, but I was in the middle of a conversation, what was I gonna do, ignore him?

"Fuck. You." I said to my dad. "You wanna hear me say it again? Fuck you. I just wanted to die. Are you happy?"

"So why don't you?" my dad asked.

"It's not that easy!"

"Well, you haven't exactly been living either, have you?"

"I don't want to be like that anymore."

"So just goddamn pick one: alive or dead?"

"I don't know."

"Alive or dead?"

"What do *you* want me to do?"

He didn't say anything, though he clearly had an opinion. Why did I even bother to ask? "Well, it's either you or your sister," he said with a shrug.

"Shut up! Shut up!" I felt tears washing down my face. It felt so unfamiliar, it took me a minute to recognize it. My guts felt terrible. If I didn't know better, I'd say they hurt.

Caitlin came running into the room in her scrubs.

"I got a page—what happened?"

Silverman pulled her aside like I couldn't hear him and told her I didn't seem hurt and that he'd already called for a psych consult.

Caitlin brushed him off and knelt down next to me.

"Quinn? What's going on?"

All I could think to say was "I'm sorry." I said it over and over.

"It's okay, just get back in bed." She tried to help me up, but I wasn't done.

"No, I'm sorry. I'm sorry about everything. I'm sorry I fucked everything up, I'm sorry I'm still even alive... Shit, I think there's something wrong with me. I feel... sick."

"Nothing's wrong with you."

"Cait, I don't *want* to die."

"You're not going to. You're gonna be okay, you're alive."

"I just don't know how to be alive without hurting people. I don't want to hurt you."

"What are you talking about?"

"Like with Mom..."

She looked me in the eye for the first time, deadly serious. "Listen to me. I am not Mom. I'm stronger than Mom. And we're going to get through this."

"I'm just...sorry." And then I just lost steam and wilted, crying like a stupid baby on my sister's shoulder. She just sat and held me, and she smelled like lemon hand soap, and I thought it had been a long time since I had been that close to her.

Silverman backed out of the room, leaving us alone. I saw, over Cait's shoulder, that Shadow Man and Demon Boy were sitting on the edge of the empty bed where my dad no longer was. Shadow Man hung his head, depressed. The boy kicked his legs back and forth like an actual little kid. I think I maybe even saw him smile.

48. Caitlin

LATER, MUCH LATER, CAITLIN stepped out of Quinn's hospital room into the fluorescent hallway. He'd finally fallen asleep in the bed with her rubbing small circles on his back, like she did for Winnie, like she remembered their mom doing for her, though never for as long as Caitlin wanted her to.

Outside it was dark, but she felt simultaneously exhausted and energized.

Will came striding down the corridor toward her, Winnie sleeping soundly in his arms, her head resting on his shoulder.

"Here you are—ready to go?" Will's voice boomed off the tile.

"Shhhh. He's sleeping." She eased the heavy door closed behind her with a dull thud. "I think I'm going to stay here awhile."

"How are you going to get home?" he asked, cranky. "The T stops running in an hour."

"I'll sleep in the on-call room."

"It's late, you can come back first thing tomorrow."

She gave him a look that settled the issue.

"Okay fine. Say goodnight." He turned his body to let Caitlin kiss Winnie, but she wasn't done talking to him yet.

"They did a psych consult today—they recommended doing a more thorough evaluation, possibly admitting him," she said.

"Really?" He tried to keep from sounding too excited.

"Yeah. But now I'm not sure."

"Why don't we talk about it tomorrow?" he said, tightly.

"What 'we'? He's my brother."

"Which is why you can't be objective about this."

"I want to give him another chance. I think this is different."

"Cait, to be honest, I'm tired of all your back and forth on this and I'm inclined to trust their opinion over yours right now."

She pounced on him, angry, "You just want him out—you were pushing for that from the start. You keep pushing to make me choose between him and you."

"Jesus, I'm just trying to hold us together." He sounded surprised by her attack, and his voice cracked with emotion. "I'm just looking out for our family."

"He's also my family."

It was a declaration, a realization, and Caitlin saw Will physically step back a bit when he heard it.

Will took a deep breath, cleared his throat, buttoned it up again. "Look, if he could get his act together, I'd have no problem with him staying. I just don't think he can."

"I want to let him know he can come home."

"I think that's the worst thing you could do."

"You don't understand—this is different, something is different, and I think he needs me."

"How do you think he got this way, Cait?"

"He was born this way."

"No, it's because of you. You never made him go to school, you never made him get a job—"

"I thought it was the best thing…"

"No one ever said you didn't have good intentions."

Will turned and walked away. Tears welled in Caitlin's eyes.

She saw how this just looked like more of the same to Will, but she knew somewhere deep inside her that it wasn't. It had been four days since she'd taken a pill—a long four days—but she was holding up. She knew it didn't work like this, knew it was verging on superstition, but she felt like Quinn could somehow sense her will to change and was meeting her challenge. She could keep up with her end of it and stay clean if she kept this idea in her mind, that she had to do it for Quinn. She couldn't share that thought with Will, though, because he didn't know about the disappearing Dilaudids, the vanishing Vicodins. Maybe she would tell him eventually, maybe when she was a little further along, when it was clear how much better things had gotten.

Caitlin watched Will disappearing down the corridor, Winnie's pale sleeping face resting like a full, rising moon on the broad horizon of his shoulder.

49. Quinn

THE THUD OF THE door closing woke me up. I sat up, a little disoriented. You know when you have a bizarre dream that still feels real when you wake up, and it takes a minute for your mind to be convinced it didn't really happen? This was like the opposite of that—something bizarre had happened that *felt* like a dream, and I had to keep reminding my brain that it had actually happened. My head was exhausted from working so hard. But I felt antsy, like something was pulling on me to get out of bed. If I was going to try to be a long-term resident on the planet, I needed to see her, I needed to face what I had done. Now.

I dragged myself over to the wheelchair, leaned on it as I eased open the heavy door, then plunked myself into the chair and rolled silently out of the room and down the corridor, past the deserted nurses' station.

"Attention all visitors, visiting hours are now officially over," a voice announced, like a stern kindergarten teacher.

I stopped outside a door toward the end of the hallway. Her door. Suddenly, I wasn't so sure this was a good idea. I heard nurse footsqueaks approaching behind me and I reacted before I could think, rolling into her room.

Just inside the door, I stopped short, caught off guard by the sight of Reese. Her sleeping, scraped-up face was peaceful underneath the alien tubes that snaked across it. Her entire left leg floated in a cast, suspended by ropes and pulleys. The room was lit only by the blue light from her roommate's television, flickering through the dividing curtain. It was a spooky sight.

I didn't want to be here. I had to be here.

I rolled over to the side of the bed and rested my cheek gently on her stomach. Tears rolled down my sideways face, tiny frictionless marbles that dropped onto her hospital gown and burst like dark fireworks.

Crying twice in one day, God, what a baby. But earlier, when the TV crashed down onto me, I felt sorry for myself because I just wanted to end it—but then I couldn't even do *that*. I had cried because I was stuck being alive, stuck hurting the people I least wanted to hurt. But now, the tears were coming because I was making myself see what had happened, what I had done to Reese. I wished I could take her place. I thought if I could feel what she felt, it might help even the score. But I knew that no wishing, praying, or begging could undo it because I had tried that all before, for my mom, and it all added up to a big fat zero.

"Attention all visitors, visiting hours are now officially over," the disembodied kindergarten teacher said again.

But I wasn't only busted up that I had done this to Reese, I was also busted up that I *cared* so much that I had, when I'd tried so hard not to. Giving a damn about anyone else opened you right up for a punch in the gut. Even as a little kid, I saw that. You couldn't be hurt if you didn't care, was my hypothesis. But my experiment was a failure. As much as I had tried to stay in my own little self-patrolled boundary, to not touch anyone and have them not touch me, it hadn't stopped people from caring about me—or me from caring about them. Or from either of us getting hurt as a result. The only choice was not to end it, but to somehow live with the risk. I couldn't not care. I couldn't not hurt. Reese was the one who had said it: "You don't get any of the good stuff in life unless you risk the bad stuff." She was right—I had to face it, even if it hurt like a mofo.

I looked up at Reese's face and it seemed for a second that her eyes might be open a bit, focused on me. I raised my head up and looked closer and decided it had probably just been the way the blue light from the TV was dancing across her face that made it look that way.

And then, footsteps.

"I know, I'm leaving. I just want to say goodnight." Donny's hulking shadow preceded him into the room. I swiveled the wheelchair around and there he was, right in front of me. He took a second to register what he was looking at, then he ripped me out of the chair and held me upright, shouting in my face.

"You got a death wish? What did I tell you about coming in here?"

He stared at me, waiting for an answer. My eyes narrowed. I knew Shadow Man would back me up like he always did, emotionless and badass. But then, something washed over me and when it drained off, so did the anger. I raised my palms in a gesture of surrender. I wasn't asking meathead Donny to spare me; I was inviting him to punish me—or at least a certain part of me. Donny wasn't a guy for subtle distinctions, but luckily it turned out that we both wanted the same thing.

He slammed me against the wall; the back of my head smacked the painted concrete blocks. I didn't fight back, I just let Donny go to town. He threw me onto the wheelchair, and it toppled over, pulling the room-dividing curtain down onto of the tangled heap of chair-plus-me.

The old woman in the other hospital bed started screaming her head off.

As Donny pulled me off the floor and continued to beat the crap out of me, I kept seeing flashes of the Shadow Man being demolished into a screaming, hurting pulp. I wasn't feeling pain, but Shadow Man was, and it didn't look good. Donny pounded on me as he yelled, "I *told* you to stay *away* from my *sister*."

"What?" Reese was now awake—though majorly drugged and confused.

A nurse came flying in the door.

"Get off of him!" She grabbed a fistful of Donny's hair and pulled him off me. I decided to just rest there where I was, in a bleeding heap on the floor.

"This is unacceptable behavior!" The nurse grabbed onto Donny's shirt and shoved him with both hands toward the door.

You can only beat up patients during visiting hours, I thought to say, but it stayed in my head because I was having a hard time getting air in my lungs. I thought it was pretty funny though.

The nurse dragged Donny out into the hall. I pulled myself over to Reese's bed.

"Hey, its me," I wheezed, "It's Quinn. Can you hear me? I just wanted to say before they make me leave that I'm sorry, I'm really sorry."

Reese opened her mouth to speak, but no sound came out. I waited, wanting to hear her blame me, be mad at me, curse at me, something, please. She tried again.

"Thank you…" she rasped.

Huh? Clearly she was too drugged up to the eyeballs to know what she was saying.

Two more nurses came in. Reese was trying to say something else.

"No talking. You just lay back and rest," said the first nurse.

The other one turned to me. "What are you doing in here? I'm sorry, you'll have to leave." I fought her, but she dumped me back into my wheelchair and rolled me out of the room while the other nurse attended to Reese.

I looked back at Reese as I was wheeled out. She was still trying to form words, and I strained to hear her as the nurse pushed me out of the room.

"You pulled me out..." she whispered. And I saw her smile at me, weakly, though her haze, as the door to her room *thunk*ed shut.

What the hell? I put some pieces together as the nurse rolled me down the hall. I peeled the bandages on my hands down and looked at my palms. Those weren't abrasions on my hands, my arms, my chest. They were burns. The grin on my face got wider and wider.

"What the heck do *you* have to be smiling about?" the nurse asked me irritably.

"Everything." I said. "Just, everything."

50. Reese

I T HURT. A LOT. Too dark to see the clock but I knew. Must be. Time for my pain meds. It hurt a lot.

The fight had woken me up, but not from much. Deep-in-the-bone pain, crunching like a river of glass shards down the length of my left leg, had kept me fitful, restless, hazy. Too unconscious to call the nurse, but not asleep enough to forget the pain. I begged the universe for sleep. Or morphine.

It seemed like a half-dream, the fight. By the time I figured out it was probably really happening, it was over. Even after, I wasn't positive. I felt the gown on my stomach. Damp with his tears. Was real.

✱

UPSIDE DOWN, SIDEWAYS, DOWNSIDE up, sideways down. The loudest sound I had ever heard. Metallic smashing and scraping. And then it stopped and I was stuck inside. Disoriented, not thinking right. Smoke and then flames. I undid my seatbelt, kicked sideways at the windshield. Nothing happened. Was there a fire extinguisher in here? Was someone coming for me?

✱

IT HURT A LOT. Where was the nurse?

Pain both split me in pieces and focused me. Made it impossible to think in a straight line, but at same time, made it necessary to think short, think clear. My body hurt, but my mind had no conflict for the first time, maybe ever. Was this why this had happened? For this? In the middle of the night, with no morphine nurse in sight, I was sure of it. It was all so clear. Had to prioritize, choose a path.

The meat smell from the hospital dinner sitting on the rolling tray in the corner assaulted me. An apple. I wanted a cold, crispy apple. No meat, ever again. I'd only been eating it at home anyway, had stopped eating it anywhere else. I was a closet vegetarian, afraid Dad would yell. Roll his eyes. Remind me it was the law of jungle. *But no more, won't eat it again*, I swore. It was a start. Volunteer at animal shelter, too? Yes. Too many cats needing help. Choose a path, do something, think clear.

✹

Nurse. Yes. She pulled a syringe from her pocket, popped open the cap to my IV and slipped it in. Pushed the plunger with her delicate thumb. Shhhh, now, she said, shhhh. Cold, metallic relief snaked up my arm, spreading joy, radiating oblivion. Her hands, so elegant, so beautiful.

He had reached in and grabbed me with his hands. His damaged hands, hands that had drawn such beautiful pictures. His hands had appeared in the window behind my head, breaking the glass with a rock, chunky crystals tumbling into my hair like heavy snow. His hands had pushed in, through flames, through jagged shards, and lifted me out. I saw them, blistering against the metal, sliced by the glass, and still coming steadily, steadily to save me. They had done something no one else could have done.

Have to believe a cat can be rehabilitated.
Hurting less, but cold.
Choose a path.
Shhhh, now.

51. Quinn

WHEN THE BONES HAD started to knit together, and the bruises had turned from purple to yellow, and the psych department decided that I was no longer a suicide risk, I was cleared to leave the hospital.

A nurse wheeled me down the hall—hospital policy—while Caitlin carried my crutches and a plastic bag with a few of my things. Just clothes and a new sketch pad that was beginning to fill with new work. But the pad looked different than any I'd ever had. There were drawings, sure—with my messed up right wrist finally in a hard cast, I'd been forced to try to use my slowly healing left, and the earliest drawings looked like a first grader's. The pen marks got surer and more confident as I'd gotten the hang of using awkward untested muscles in my hand and brain. But in the margins, swirling around and beside the drawings, filling the blank space on every page, were words. Crabbed, hard-fought words. Notes to self. Making sense out of disorder. Drawing the forest. Page one: "I got hit by a car on the day my dad died."

�҉

As I WAS PUSHED past the open door to Reese's room, I craned my neck and caught a glimpse of Donny and Mr. R sitting at the foot of her bed. Quiet. Mute football on the overhead TV. Waiting for the slow miracle.

On the wall, across from her bed, were the drawings I had snuck in and taped there, one each night as she slept, drawings of her, each one more competent, each one more finished, each one more healed. Drawing her back to health.

✠

IN THE CAR—A TINY, tinny rental that was doing duty until the insurance check arrived and they could buy a new used one—Cait and I rode home in silence.

The morning sun radiated off the glass of the Hancock Tower in Copley Square, the shiny skyscraper looming over the dignified stonework of Trinity Church. Worker bees scurried from the subway stop to their offices, carrying cooling coffees, laptops, better shoes—worrying about all the wrong things, it seemed to me. As Cait drove along the winding riverbank, I saw college scullers skimming along like water bugs, and a homeless man pushing a shopping cart stockpile. The world, I thought. Different for everyone, and the same for everyone. Hard and easy. Sad and hopeful. All at once. Maybe the key was trying to remember that whatever it seemed to be, it was also the opposing thing, every day, all the time.

When Caitlin pulled the car up outside their house and turned off the engine, neither one of us moved for a long time. I wondered if she was regretting her decision.

We both glanced up and saw Will standing in the kitchen window, looking out at us. He and Caitlin held each other's gaze for a long time, neither of them giving away a hint of emotion. I just watched them looking at each other for a minute until he turned away and disappeared into the darkness of the house. I didn't know what agreement they had come to, but I was pretty sure he wasn't throwing me a welcome home party.

Cait sighed, and after a moment, we both spoke at the same time. Just as I said "Cait, listen," she said, "Quinn?"

"What?" she asked first.

"No, go ahead, what were you going to say?"

"Nothing. Go on."

"Just… I think this is going to be a temporary thing. Here with you," I said.

"Really? If that's what you want…"

"I think it is."

"Okay."

"No offense."

"No, it's okay." She got out of the car.

"What were you going to say?" I asked.

"I don't remember," she said, already halfway up the front stairs, halfway smiling. Yes, she had given me chances before, but this somehow felt different to me, and I really thought it seemed like it felt different to her too. She went in the front door, leaving it open for me.

I straggled out of the car with my crutches, pushed the car door shut with the rubber tip of the right one. Across the street, in the schoolyard, the gang of kids piled on top of the same poor Scrawny Kid who I'd seen getting beat up before.

"Hey, leave the damn kid alone!" I shouted.

Stunned, the kids stared at me, then scattered. The victim stood and brushed the pebbles and dirt off the front of his clothes.

"Hey, thanks," he called across the street to me.

"Shut up," I grumbled.

I pivoted on my crutches and followed Caitlin up the stairs and into the house.

52. Quinn

I NEVER NOTICED THIS BENCH while I was walking by, or during the time I worked at the butcher shop. It's right across the street from the front door of the shop. Just a wooden bench where a million butts have sat while waiting for a bus or a friend. The armrests are metal, and in pretty good shape, but the wooden slats of the back and seat are gouged with names, initials, curse words. Maybe Isabella really *was* a slut, I can't say, but someone felt strongly enough about it to spend an hour making sure the neighborhood knew. I wonder if Isabella has sat on this bench, has seen those words. If she's moved away by now. If she's now a mom, a grandmother, an investment banker. Maybe she even moved because of this bench.

I almost feel like I know this Isabella girl, because I've been sitting next to her name for a long time, watching the buses come and go. It would have been a great time to smoke some cigs, except I gave them up after the accident. Other things have changed too—like for instance, since I started drawing again, my characters have totally stopped following me around. Haven't seen 'em once.

So I'm sitting here on this bench, doing some noodling in my sketchbook, drawing and writing down the stuff I just told you about Isabella, but nothing too serious, because I can't fully concentrate. I'm keeping an eye out for Reese. Cait checked for me, so I know she got out of the hospital more than a month ago, but I haven't seen her. I don't have a number for her. And

I don't want to go inside the shop. So I've been coming to the bench all week to take my chances.

I know it's crazy, but I don't know what else to do. I've been here a couple of hours this morning, and just as I'm thinking about going down the block to get some coffee or something, it happens. I see her. A couple of times before, I saw someone who I thought might be her from down the block, but then it tuned out I was wrong. But this time, I immediately fully know that it's her, no doubt. She's swinging along on crutches, her leg still in a cast, next to a girlfriend, who's carrying both their backpacks. She doesn't see me, and I just watch her approach with her friend. Something's different, and it takes me a minute to realize that she's wearing normal clothes. I've never seen her without some crazy outfit, and normal almost seems like a costume on her. But I like it.

She and her friend stop in front of the shop, chatting and smiling. They finally say goodbye, and the friend gives Reese her backpack and leaves. As Reese turns to open the door of the shop, she spots me staring at her from across the street. I search her face for clues, but her expression is neutral. For a second, I think maybe she has amnesia. Maybe she's forgotten me and we can start over. But as I limp across the street to meet her—the bones of my broken ankle fused so it doesn't flex anymore when I walk—she suddenly bursts into tears.

"Oh my god," I hurry over to her as quickly as I can, "What's wrong?"

"Nothing," she says, "It's not… I'm not sad… It's good crying, I'm sorry…" She smiles a big smile and throws her arms around me in a tight hug. "I'm glad you're okay, I'm glad I'm okay."

I don't really know what to say. My face feels hot. "Okay good," I say quietly into her neck, "I thought maybe you'd lost your cat again."

She steps back, blinking the tears away and wiping her sniffly nose with her sleeve. "How long have you been standing out here?" she asks.

"Four days." I round down, not counting the partial days when I just came by for an hour or two.

"I'm not working here anymore."

"I sort of figured that out."

"I just come and help my dad out on Fridays."

"Good thing, or I might have been standing here till spring." She smiles at my attempt at humor, but then there's silence as we just stand there and look at each other. *Shit, am I blowing it? This is kind of like starting over. Say something...think, think...*

"How are you?" *Did that just come out of my mouth? That's genius, you idiot. The most mundane thing you possibly could have said...* But she tilts her head and gives me a tiny, startled smile, like she's a little surprised that I asked. And I realize I probably never have really asked anyone that question before. I guess mundane is okay sometimes, if you mean it.

"I'm okay. You?"

I go for broke. "I'm okay, too. Good, even. I'm working on finishing my book, and I think I might have gotten some work—a friend of mine showed some of my drawings to a guy and it looks like he's gonna give me a chance on an illustration job. I want to start saving up for my own place, get out of my sister's hair."

"Wow," she nods, taking this in.

"You're going to school?" I ask. Keep it on her.

"Yeah. Just two classes at the community college. Thinking I'll try to transfer to BU when I'm ready. Next year probably."

"That's great."

More silence.

"Hey, isn't that your dog?"

My heart stops for half a beat as I see what she's pointing to. It's the Black Dog, trotting down the sidewalk like a normal everyday frickin' dog.

"He, uh…he just used to follow me around. He was never really mine."

"He's cute—you should take him home." She bends down and makes kissy sounds toward the dog. "Come here, baby, are you lost?"

"Just leave him alone." The dog cruises past us, without even a pause, or a glance toward me. He keeps going, jogging off around the corner, out of sight. "He'll probably just go back to where he came from," I say.

"Well…I really should go in and help my dad." She glances over at the shop. "I mean, I told him and Donny what you did, but still…I don't think Donny really…"

"I get it. That's cool. Can we maybe see each other soon?"

"Yeah. Do you want my number?" She pulls out her cell phone.

"Um, I've never had a phone. But you know what, I'll get one, and the only number I'll put in it is yours."

She looks over her shoulder into the shop again and I follow her look and see her dad watching us from behind the counter. "Ok, then. I'm gonna… I'd better go," she says, turning to go inside, awkwardly holding both crutches in one hand as she reaches for the door.

"Hey, wait, I got you something." I reach into my bag and pull out my gift, an oddly shaped cylinder, wrapped terribly with tissue paper and surgical tape.

"No, really, you don't have to…" She waves me off.

"Please take it." I hold it out to her, my arm like half a bridge. It hangs there for eons, as she seems to debate whether to take it or not.

I think she realizes I am not going to pull my hand back, ever, so she finally reaches out and takes it.

"Thank you," I say, so quiet I can barely hear myself. I back away as she unwraps it. It's nothing special, just one of those big prayer candles you can get off the bottom shelf of the last row of any little corner grocery. It's got a portrait of Saint Margaret on it.

Reese reads the type off the back of the candle, "'Saint Margaret is often invoked by those with kidney disease and women in childbirth?'"

"It was the closest thing to a 'get well' saint I could find." There's nothing else I can say. That was why I had come, so I just turn to go before I can blurt out something really dumb. I limp off down the street. Reese crutches into the shop. Both of us moving slowly, with our crooked, messed-up bodies.

I turn around and stand there for a minute, watching her go, and it suddenly flashes into my mind. The ending of my graphic novel, all of it. I see the cover of the finished book displayed in the window of Steve's Komix, kids lined up to buy it. I see Demon Boy, now grown-up, as a Human Torch–like superhero who could control his powers—and who looks a lot like a slacker teenager in his regular life—yeah, yeah, sorta like me, sure. Shadow Man has been defeated, banished. And I see a new character, Transformer Girl—a female character that maybe, sort of, slightly resembles Reese… Her super powers allow her to assume any appearance, as long as it's got style, of course. And finally, I see the last panel. Demon Boy and Transformer Girl walking off into a crazy, blazing sunset together.

I really am ready to be done with that story, on account of this new one I've already got going on. Like I said before, I wasn't just talking to talk. I told you about everything that happened because I had to. Because I needed to make some sense of it all. And if I wrote it down and didn't show it to you, it wouldn't work. Damn it if my whackadoodle art teacher wasn't right.

I keep watching as Reese finally maneuvers her crutches over the threshold of the shop door and reaches back with one arm to close it. *Come on, do it—come on, do it.* And then she does: she glances back at me. I bust into a big goofy grin—I just can't help it. And she gives me the greatest half smile in return. Half is more than enough. Half is hope.

End.